Counsel for the Defense

and Other Stories

Counsel for the Defense

and Other Stories

Lia Matera

Five Star
Unity, Maine

Five Star First Edition Mystery series.

Published in 2000 in conjunction with
Tekno-Books and Ed Gorman.

Cover photograph by Smith & Powers.

Set in 11 pt. Plantin by Rick Gundberg.

Printed in the United States on permanent paper.

Library of Congress Cataloging-in-Publication Data

Matera, Lia.
   Counsel for the defense and other stories / by
Lia Matera. — 1st ed.
      p.   cm.
   Contents: Counsel for the defense — Destroying angel — Easy
go — Do not resuscitate — The river mouth — Performance crime
— Dead drunk — If it can't be true — Dream lawyer.
   ISBN 0-7862-2537-8 (hc : alk. paper)
   1. Detective and mystery stories, American. 2. Legal stories,
American. I. Title.
PS3563.A83537 C68   2000
   813′.54—dc21
                                        00-024237

TABLE OF CONTENTS

INTRODUCTION

Many writers begin their careers with short stories, eventually moving on to novels. But I had already published four of my twelve books before attempting a story. And in the subsequent decade, I produced only nine. There's a reason for this: short stories are much too hard to write! They contain nearly a novel's worth of plot with none of the elbow room. Characters must be introduced, established, and understood within paragraphs, and every line of dialog and exposition does double-duty creating misdirection and suspense. I've worked nearly as long on some short stories as I have on first drafts of novels.

In fact, a few of these stories began as novels about personal relationships between lawyers and clients. I am a recovering lawyer myself, which is why the protagonists of my two series, Willa Jansson and Laura Di Palma, are attorneys.

"Counsel for the Defense," for example, reached book length before I realized I was dissatisfied with it as a novel. After much paring and rethinking, it became my first short story. In it, a lawyer defends her ex-husband against a murder charge, all the while using her power over him to exact revenge for his infidelity years ago. "Easy Go," which also began as a novel, shows a lawyer chafing as she's forced to work for her former fiancé. And "Dream Lawyer," another drastically cut-down book (the only one featuring characters from both my series), is about the limits of what an attorney can do for her clients. Like my novels, these stories are about lawyers stepping into their clients' tragedies—amplifying them, being compromised by them, suffering by association with them. I wasn't able for various reasons to shape these into novels, but invitations from anthology editors gave me a chance to prune and smooth them into what you find here.

Other short stories have given me welcome breaks from writing about lawyers. "Destroying Angel," in which a fungus expert is wrongly accused of serving poison mushrooms, and "The River Mouth," where travelers mistake veiled threats for local lore, allowed me to say something about the wild world outside the courtroom—or any room. "Do Not Resuscitate," about a second wife's jealousy when her husband's dying words are about her predecessor, and "Performance crime," where a woman tries hard to be "politically correct" about crime, are character studies of women very unlike my usual protagonists. I think of these stories as work furloughs.

The other two stories in this collection are harder for me to pigeonhole. Though "Dead Drunk" features a lawyer, she is really acting as a private investigator, trying to learn who is pouring water over passed-out drunks so they'll freeze to death on winter nights. I was delighted when this story won the Private Eye Writers of America Shamus Award for best short story of 1996.

As to "If It Can't Be True," well . . . every once in a while, a writer just has to go out on a slender limb. My crime novels are usually about lapses in political and personal values. But this story deals with an apparently supernatural event slamming a family hard against the limits of conventional wisdom.

Though I am not a writer who finds short stories easy or quick to write, I don't regret spending nearly a novel's worth of time on some of these. And given my frequent vow never to attempt another, I am truly delighted to have this opportunity to collect here all the stories I've written so far.

Counsel for the Defense

"I'm your lawyer," I reminded him, in much the same tone I'd used in the not so distant past to say, "I'm your wife."

Jack Krauder glowered at the acrylic partition separating us from a yawning jailer. "Howard Frost is my lawyer."

"And Howard Frost is my associate—my *junior* associate. You hired a law firm, Jack, not a person."

"I asked for Howard."

"He's in court. I'm not." And I'm a better lawyer, anyway. "Through the miracle of modern science"—I fiddled with a small tape recorder—"Howie can hear everything you tell me. *If* you make up your mind to tell me what happened."

"You don't believe me." His voice was carefully uninflected; a contractor's trick he'd perfected on angry homeowners and stubborn zoning boards.

"You lived with Mary Sutter for how long? Six months?" Seven months and nine days, to be exact. "You must know something. More than what's in here." I tapped the police report. "Remember how I used to complain about my clients lying by omission? Ransilov, remember him? Leaving me open to that surprise about . . . Jack?" I slid a sympathetic hand across the gouged metal table that separated us. "Don't booby-trap your own defense."

Jack released the arm of his chair, dropping his hand onto the table like a piece of meat. He frowned at his chafed red knuckles, apparently unable to will the hand to touch mine. Two years of connubial hell will do that to a relationship.

"Okay, Jack, let's try this: Mary tries to kill you and kill herself, but something goes wrong. You don't drink your coffee and she drinks hers. She dies and you don't."

His hand formed a fist. "No."

"What's the alternative? Someone hated Mary—or you—enough to kill you both. Someone close enough to know where you keep your coffee."

He looked at the dirty salmon walls, at the mesh-caged fluorescent lights, at the chipped expanse of metal table—at everything in the room except me. His dimpled jaw was tense enough to use as an anvil.

"That's it, isn't it? And you know who did it, don't you? Don't you, Jack?"

He pounded the table once, meeting my eye. "Don't try to bully me, Janet."

"I just want the truth."

There it was, the bare bones of the quarrel that had blown our marriage out of the water.

"Okay, Jack. Your bail hearing is tomorrow afternoon. I'll make the arrangements—"

"No!" he exploded.

"What do you mean, 'no'? It could be six, eight months until your trial. You can't stay here."

"Goddammit—I can if I want to. I'll discuss it with Howard."

"Jack. I know you don't want to go back to—Look, you can stay at my place."

"No."

"Or a hotel. Anyplace is better than the county—"

He stood abruptly, turning his back on me. "Leave me alone, Janet."

As the sheriff's deputy led him out of the room, Jack glanced back at me. My ex-husband looked worried.

10

★ ★ ★ ★ ★

Jack's kitchen table, his counter, his back door were still dusty with fingerprint powder. Traces of chalk defaced the hardwood floor. Judging by the outline, Mary Sutter had died in a heap. Strychnine. The coroner said she'd convulsed violently enough to break two bones.

Howard Frost sighed deeply, polishing his camera lens. I'm a better photographer than Howie, but I didn't offer to take the pictures. Not this time.

"Lived here yourself once, did you?" Howie's English-accented voice was bland, as usual. A handicap in court.

"All this crap"—I indicated the cozy Americana, the maple table, the enamel-topped hutch, the rocker in the corner—"I picked it out."

"Mmm." He put the camera to his eye, twisting the focus, leaning closer to the graphite-dusted table. A cross-hatching of clean squares indicated where police tape had lifted prints.

I turned to the hutch. The drawers had already been rummaged. Old contracting bids, wholesalers' receipts for sheetrock, receipts for Mary's art supplies, unmailed Publishers Clearing House envelopes, one of them addressed to me. "I wonder if the cops know this thing has a false bottom." I cleared the jumbled papers to one side, feeling for the catch.

Behind me Howie mused, "Poisoning coffee right in the canister." A tinge of outrage; the most I'd ever heard in that well-modulated voice. "Bloody reckless. Suppose they'd had company?"

"Jack's lucky. I've never met a bigger caffeine addict. What are the odds of him being late for work and having to skip his morning cup—" The false bottom came loose. "Jesus, Howie. Look at this."

I held up a photograph. It showed a young woman lying splay-legged beside a swimming pool, her hair wet and her eyes lost behind big sunglasses. At first glance the woman appeared to be Mary Sutter, but Mary's hair had been waist-length; in the photo the damp straggles barely reached her shoulders. Also, Mary had been gaunt and proud of her wrinkly, sun-baked hide. The woman in the photo had a plumper, more youthful figure. ♪

There were two men with her, one lying down, one squatting. Both of them rippled with beautiful muscles. Young, Latino, dark hair and eyes, possibly brothers. All three wore suggestive smiles and nothing else. They might have been sunbathing; or they might have been doing something more interesting.

Howie stepped up behind me. "Strange the police missed it."

I let the false bottom fall back into place. "Just like in the movies. Only I wonder . . ." I considered the photo. "A younger Mary Sutter? Wouldn't it be great if someone was blackmailing her? Talk about injecting reasonable doubt into the prosecution's case."

"Dunno. Pretty tame stuff, this. And no reason Jacko should keep quiet about somebody blackmailing Mary. Not anymore."

I turned to face him. His baby-smooth skin was unusually pale as he regarded the photo.

"Jacko" had recently joined Howie's soccer team. It had been something of a trial, these last months, hearing my coworker praise Jack's "trapping." (Howie was *my* associate, *my* friend. Bad enough Jack got the house and the furniture.)

"I wasn't married to Jack Krauder two years too many without knowing when he's holding back. There's more to this—" I put the picture down on the powdered enamel. "I have a bad feeling about this picture, Howie. Like I'm standing over a trapdoor."

12

"Janet? I really would be happy to talk to him. Tonight? Or before my trial tomorrow?"

"I'll take care of it." How many times did I have to explain? "If we want information, we're going to have to shake it out of him. Jack needs management—not friendship."

I'd never liked Carole Bissett, not from the moment she'd moved next door to me and Jack. An aerobics instructor, just my luck. Jack's luck, rather: Fortune always surrounded him with beautiful women. (I had been the exception.) I couldn't prove it, but I suspected Jack had been sleeping with Carole through most of the last year of our marriage. She was one of the reasons I'd let him keep the house; I loathed the sight of Carole's shiny spandex.

She dabbed her glowing cheeks with a terry wristband and pulled two bottles of Evian water out of her refrigerator. "Poor Jackie. I wish I could help him."

I took one of the bottles, wishing it had about three fingers of whiskey in it. "Maybe you can. Did you notice anything unusual next door, odd comings and goings, people you wouldn't expect to see?"

Carole wrinkled her darling little nose. "Well, you know artists. Lots of Mary's friends were kind of weird." Then, remorsefully, "I shouldn't talk bad about her."

"Any drugs?"

A tolerant smile. "Nothing hard, but sure. Mary smoked a little and did a few lines. Jackie doesn't—you know him."

"Where did Mary get it?"

She hesitated. "I don't want to get anyone in trouble."

"Jack's in a lot of trouble." Carole's brain was certainly her least used muscle. "Was it those two good-looking Chicano guys—what were their names?"

"Jaime and Andy?" Her face contorted with the effort of

thinking. Come on, I urged silently; no pain, no gain.
"Maybe."

"Know where I can find them?"

"Try Stacy. They came over with her most of the time."

"Stacy?"

"Mary's kid sister."

Once again I stared at Jack across the metal table. Square
of face, green eyes, black hair spilling over his forehead like
Superman's—so damned handsome. Too bad about the divorce. Look where it had gotten him. Look where it had
gotten me, for that matter.

"I know about Stacy now, Jack."

His expression grew wary. "What about her?"

"Nice try—*Jackie*. But I've been to see her." Been to see
her, and been turned away at the door by a harried woman in
a nurse's slack-suit. Apparently Stacy Sutter was taking her
sister's death hard. Maybe she had good reason.

"I thought I'd better follow up on the snapshot I found in
your hutch drawer. Under the false bottom."

"What snapshot?"

"The little orgy by your pool, naked kids and some
unclassic coke."

His lips compressed to a white line, his eyes narrowed to
glinting slits.

"Want to know what the picture says to me? One of two
things: Either you and Mary were paying blackmailers to
keep the negative private—and no one would want a picture
like that made public, not even someone like Stacy Sutter."

Jack's' nostrils began to flare, he was getting angrier.

"Or, second possibility: pornographic thrills for you.
Nude girl young enough to be your daughter."

He was almost angry enough now.

14

"Then there's the drug angle. Stacy's addicted to cocaine. The two men in the picture are pushers."

I thought I had him, but he choked back what he meant to say.

"Look, Jack, you can protect Stacy Sutter if you want to. Maybe it doesn't matter to you that she killed Mary and tried to kill you. But I wonder what you did to make her so angry? Or was sleeping with both sisters enough?"

He stood, his chair toppling over backward. His face mottled, his hands shook.

The jailer immediately ran in, pinning him in a choke hold.

"You haven't changed a bit!" Jack hissed at me.

I paced around the office in my stocking feet. Howie lay on my couch, eyes closed.

"Here's my theory," I said. "Jack's sleeping with Stacy Sutter. She gets morbid about cheating with her sister's boyfriend and tries to kill both of them. Jack feels responsible and decides to keep his mouth shut for Stacy's sake."

"Bit of a stretch. Hard to imagine Jacko—or anybody—being so chivalrous."

"Not chivalrous—conventional. Conventional enough to feel like he's got it coming for sleeping with both—"

"You never seemed to find him too, um, 'conventional' when you were married to him."

Tactful Howie. "If you mean *faithful,* no. I'd never accuse him of that. But he's definitely a home-and-family kind of man; marrying me when we thought I was—Buying that house for us. There's a big difference between sleeping with a neighbor, which is a traditionally macho kind of thing to do"—I made a conscious effort to eliminate bitterness from my voice—"and sleeping with your lover's baby sister. And, Howie, you should have seen his reaction when I asked him about it. The veins in his neck practically exploded."

"No doubt." Howie rubbed his knuckles over a clean-shaven cheek. "But where does it leave us? Assuming Jack won't admit it and the baby sister won't, either?"

"Jaime and Andy."

"Beg your pardon?"

"The two men in the picture with Stacy Sutter. They supplied Mary with drugs. They were obviously in Stacy's pants, and maybe in her confidence too. Odds are they knew about Stacy and Jack." I crossed to my desk. "The trouble is, drug dealers are damned lousy witnesses."

"Easily impeached," Howie agreed.

"Vindictive too." Last time we'd subpoenaed a coke dealer, he'd put our client in the hospital.

"You don't suppose . . . ?" There was an uncharacteristic hesitancy in Howie's voice. "You're thinking Jacko'd rot in jail to protect a woman. Have you wondered if he might be guilty?"

I slipped my pumps on. "Can you imagine a more acrimonious divorce than ours, Howie? If Jack didn't kill *me*"—I shrugged—"he doesn't have it in him."

Howie blinked up at me. "Funny he'd want you to represent him."

"Well, he does." Too defensive. I looked away. Outside my window, a billboard advertised KATY'S KOFFEE KUP, KOUNTRY BREAKFAST AND MMMM MMMM KOFFEE.

Let Howard learn the truth from Jack, later. By then I'd have Jack out, maybe have things resolved.

"See, Howie"—I laughed nervously—"when we were married, I used to toot my own horn all the time, tell Jack I was the best criminal lawyer in the state. Just to impress him, you know how it is."

"Mmm." I heard a whisper of amusement, Howie knew I believed it. "And the, um, history doesn't . . . *disturb* him?"

"Oh hell, of course it disturbs him." I began checking the contents of my briefcase. "He's guarded with me. Prickly. Probably thinks I still resent him leaving me for Mary." I bit my lip, rearranging my papers. "And maybe I do, a little." I let the briefcase lid slam down. "But Jack can't do any better than me, and at some level he knows it." Why else would he ask for my junior associate? They were friends, sure, but my name came first on the letterhead. "What I'm really afraid of—" I rubbed my breastbone; it was hot in the room, hard to breathe. "He doesn't want to post bail, Howie. He won't even discuss it."

Howard sat up, brows puckering. "Feeling too battered to care what happens to him? Life without Mary . . . ?"

Mary! I stuffed my fists into my pockets. "I wonder if he—? You don't suppose he *wants* to stay inside?" Refusing to discuss his defense, sticking to a bare outline of events. "Howie, he couldn't *want* to stay in jail, could he?"

Howie tilted his head, considering. /

"Or . . . What if he *expects* us to screw up?" Hiring an inexperienced kid to represent him—his ex-wife's employee. Maybe it wasn't a vote of confidence. Maybe it was sabotage. "He *can't* think I'd screw up on purpose?"

Howie was silent. The possibility had occurred to him. "You know I wouldn't."

"Janet? If he does want to stay inside? Could he be protecting himself?"

"From what? How much lower can you go than the county bedbug farm?"

"Six feet under?" Howie squinted at the window; *Mmmm Mmmm Koffee*, the billboard promised. "Someone tried to kill him. Perhaps he feels safer behind bars right now."

"Safer? Kiddo, prisoners are murdered in their cells every day of the—" I turned away, shaken. "Where the hell's my jacket?" ⸲

I got to the county jail half an hour before Jack's bail hearing. As the sheriff's deputy and I approached the short row of cells, I could hear someone retching, a drunk singing, voices speaking Spanish. I hoped Jack felt crowded enough to reconsider posting bail.

When I saw the other prisoners, I gripped the deputy's arm and pointed. "What are *they* doing here?"

The deputy brushed my hand off his arm. "Processed a few hours ago. Cocaine. Possession for sale."

For a moment I stared at the two handsome Latinos. The drunk stopped singing to leer at me. I scanned the remaining cells for Jack. He was lying prone in the cell between the drunk and the Latinos. His face was turned to the wall.

"Jesus! They've *killed* him!"

The deputy looked at me as if I were insane, especially after Jack rolled over and sat up.

I leaned back against the wall, one hand over my heart. "Listen, those two men knew Mary Sutter—they sold her drugs. They might have been blackmailing her sister."

The young Latinos watched quizzically. The taller one murmured something in Spanish to the other.

Jack sputtered, "What the hell are you talking about?"

"The trouble is, you don't care if they kill you, do you, Jack? You won't give me the facts I need to acquit you, but you don't want to spend your life behind bars." Not the sort of thing a lawyer should say in public, but I couldn't stop. "Well, I'm not going to let you stay here and get murdered."

The deputy stepped between me and the bars. "Nobody's getting murdered in my jail."

18

"Nobody *else,* you mean?"

A month earlier a drug dealer had died in his cell on the eve of testifying against a codefendant. Neighboring prisoners hadn't "noticed" the dealer's head crack open on the bars between the cells. The sheriff had called it accidental death, a case of slip and fall.

I'd seen the body in a steel drawer. If the man slipped, he'd done it half a dozen times.

The deputy turned purple.

"Your Honor, not only is there no risk of flight in this case, but I believe the defendant is actually in physical, mortal danger if he remains in the county facility."

There were reporters behind me in the pew-like seats. I could hear excited whispers. I could feel the district attorney's fury, the judge's crotchety distaste for melodrama. But I didn't seem to have much choice. I explained about Jaime and Andy, handing the judge and the D.A. each a copy of the photograph I'd found in Jack's hutch. "These two men are now in the cell beside Mr. Krauder's, Your Honor. I believe they arranged their own arrest in order to kill my client before his trial."

The judge pounded his gavel to silence the spectators.

"Your Honor." The district attorney sounded predictably skeptical. "We'll be challenging the admissibility—and the relevance—of this photograph at another time, but I should state for the record that I have personal knowledge of the two men to whom counsel refers. Their names are Julio and Silvio Marcos. They were arrested for possession of narcotics on a tip from a reliable source."

Reliable source—that's police code for any anonymous slimeball who phones them.

"At the very least"—I struggled to keep calm—"they

should be placed in another facility until bail is posted."

"I've never seen those men before." Jack volunteered. "They're not Jaime and Andy."

The judge, a sour old prune, glared at me. "Then I see little point in making special arrangements to separate these prisoners, do you, Miss Dale?"

I never thought I'd hear myself say it about my own client. "He's lying, Your Honor."

The D.A. all but gasped.

"Approach the bench," the judge barked. His tone said, Out to the woodshed with you, young lady.

I gripped the oak rim of the judge's bench and craned my neck to entreat him. "Please. I don't want to give away the details of my defense, Your Honor, but those two men are involved—"

The D.A. slapped the photograph I'd handed him. "These are different men. Even Krauder says—"

"The sun's behind them. Look more closely. They're the same—"

"Janet." The D.A. and I had faced each other in court too often to remain mere acquaintances. "I know you used to be married to the guy, but you're being paranoid here."

Furious, I turned away from him. "Your Honor, it won't hurt to separate these men from—"

"Enough!" The judge thumped his blotter with a wizened hand. "This is not Los Angeles. You are well aware that we have only one facility here. And I am certainly not going to jeopardize the proceedings against these two men by busing them upstate, Miss Dale."

I could see from his face that further comment was useless. I glanced at the D.A. His air of concern was humiliating.

I stalked back to counsel's table. Jack's mouth twisted into a frosty sneer. He said loudly, "This woman isn't my lawyer. I don't want her representing me."

The judge barked, "What? Miss Dale, did the defendant authorize you to state an appearance?"

I forced myself to look away from Jack. Idiot! "My associate, Howard Frost, is defendant's counsel of record, Your Honor. Mr. Frost couldn't be here this afternoon. He's in trial, and I'm filling in—"

"Then I don't want bail." Jack's voice seethed with malice. "I'd rather stay where I am until—"

"Shut up, Jack!"

More commotion in the pews. The judge shouted with exasperation, "Miss Dale, why are you wasting this court's time with a bail hearing if your client—Mr. Frost's client—does not wish—" He rapped the gavel several times. "Quiet! All of you! This is not a ball game, this is a court of law."

There was very little doubt in my mind that with his next breath the judge would order Jack escorted back to his cell. I looked at Jack and hated him for what he was forcing me to do.

"I won't be a party to Mr. Krauder's indirect suicide, Your Honor," I insisted. "That's what you're asking me to do." I spoke louder, over the judge's fierce cry that I was in contempt of his court. "Jack knows he'll get killed in jail, and he doesn't care. He feels morally responsible. He wants to protect—" I gulped. I was losing control, I mustn't do that. "You'd have to know Jack to understand. Someone he cares about, someone he thinks he's wronged, is involved with drug dealers—with these two prisoners, Jaime and Andy. Don't you see, they're afraid Jack's going to implicate them . . ."

I looked around the courtroom. The judge's livid outrage, the D.A.'s shocked pity. . . hysterical ex-wife, that's what they were thinking. And I was remembering last month's dead prisoner, with his broken, bloody forehead.

In a moment the proceeding would be declared over, and

Jack would be whisked away. I played my trump card.

Jack's lips parted, then his jaw dropped. "Damn," he whispered, looking down the barrel of a revolver I'd just pulled from my briefcase.

I saw the district attorney motion to the bailiff, and I swung the gun toward him instinctively before deciding it was safer to keep it trained on one person. And because I was taking him with me, that person had to be Jack.

"Please," I begged the judge. "Try to understand why I'm doing this. If it turns out the prisoners aren't Jaime and Andy, okay. I'll bring Jack back. But I can't risk his going back in there and getting killed."

There was a charged silence as the judge raised his arms. For a moment he was motionless, a robed scarecrow. Then he croaked, "Keep the aisles clear, please. I do not want the defendant endangered by any act of ours."

"I won't go," Jack growled. He lowered his head bullishly, eyes on the gun.

I extended my arms until the gun was inches from his face: Careful, *toro.* "I'm throwing my career down the toilet for you, Jack. My *career.* To save your miserable life. Cooperate with me for once, goddammit."

The hand that held the gun was steady. I'd won trophies for marksmanship; I hoped Jack remembered them. After what seemed a span of years, he turned and led the way out of the courtroom.

Spectators stirred, a flash cube popped. My hand remained steady. No one got heroic.

The corridors were nearly empty. I'd asked for a late-afternoon hearing. The clerk of the court, a woman carrying a Danish, a lawyer slumped on a Naugahyde bench; they watched in pale alarm, making no move to interfere. We made it to my car, illegally parked beside the back entrance. I squealed out of the lot, checking for cruisers. Most of them were still across town, responding to a false alarm I'd phoned in before the hearing. I drove with one hand, bracing the muzzle of the gun against Jack's crotch.

"Don't try to grab it, Jack. If it goes off, you won't be dead, but you'll be awfully unhappy."

I glanced at him. He was as white as tapioca. His eyes were closed, as if in prayer.

It was imperative to ditch the car; the cops would soon have my license plate number. I pulled into an underground parking garage. I was lucky, there was no one down there. I didn't have to worry about concealing the gun as I motioned Jack out of the car and into the elevator.

We got out at the top and found ourselves alone on a windy roof. Jack backed ten, fifteen, feet away from me before I raised the gun again. "Let's start over, *Jackie*. No more bullshit. Tell me what you know."

"This is only a four-story building. The fall might not kill me."

"The fall," I repeated.

"That's what you have in mind, isn't it? You'll say I confessed to the murder and jumped off in remorse. You'll say you tried to stop me, but I overpowered you. You'll cry about how much you loved me, and everyone will believe you because you were willing to be disbarred for me." His face twisted with contempt, and for the first time I felt my gun hand tremble. "Tell you what I know? I know you tricked me into marrying you and almost strangled me with your clinging and complaining. You were jealous of every woman I ever said hello to, and our divorce didn't change that one bit. You think I didn't see you spying on me and Mary? You and your damn telephoto lens. You took that picture of Stacy and her friends at our pool, didn't you? Thinking it was Mary."

The distance between us seemed to increase. "No."

"You say you found it at my house. If you did, you planted it there."

"Why would I do that?"

"So the police would believe you thought Jaime and Andy were in jail with me. You know damn well those two guys aren't Jaime and Andy. Hell, *you* probably got them busted. Your job puts you in contact with every drug dealer in town. All you had to do was choose two who looked a little like the picture and call the cops on them."

"Why should I—?"

"So you'd have a reason to do this: Get me out of jail and finish the job you started when you poisoned the coffee."

I looked at him across the sooty expanse of roof. Broad of chest, long-legged, black hair blowing—handsome damn bastard.

"You managed to sink some of my relationships, didn't you, Janet? I've often wondered what you said to my accountant to make her quit like that. But you could see that Mary and I—" He kneaded his chest as though it ached. "We were too much in love to let you come between us. And you couldn't stand it. You were going to kill both of us. But I skipped coffee that morning. And you know I'm not stupid. Sooner or later I was bound to see you'd done it. You're the only person I know who's crazy enough. I just wish to Christ I'd realized—I've had so much to deal with—" He slid both hands through his hair, gripping his head, rounding his shoulders. "I thought you were just being *you*. Until you pulled the gun, I didn't—"

"I love you, Jack." If only he'd let me comfort him.

"Love!" The word vibrated with loathing. His arms snapped to his sides like a soldier's. "You'd have killed me when I got out on bail, wouldn't you? Who'd suspect my lawyer? And when I told you I didn't want to post bail, you had to arrange this little charade. Planting that photograph, getting those chicanos busted, the scene you played in front of the jailer so you could get his testimony later. And, of course, 'rescuing' me today. Maybe you'll get disbarred for it, but there's gonna be a lot of sympathy for you, too—even when they find out you were 'wrong' about those two guys in jail. You'll have a little breakdown, probably quite sincere, over my death. And your pal the D.A. will go easy on you. You might not even do any time—hell, if anyone knows all the angles, it's you."

"You shouldn't have left me, Jack. Mary didn't love you like I do."

He spat at me.

"Fine, you *bastard!* Jump or be shot. Take your pick."

"What'll you tell them if you shoot me?"

"That you came at me to kill me."

"After confessing?"

I nodded.

"Well, it won't work, Janet. There's a witness." He pointed behind me.

And sure enough, there was Howie Frost, face crinkled in astonishment. "Janet?" He shook his head, not quite convinced it was happening. "My trial's in recess—I got their expert disqualified."

Well, well, he was learning. "I stepped outside and saw your car at the rear entrance. And knowing how you feel about Jacko . . . I thought I'd better pull my car up behind, keep an eye on it." Howie hugged himself. "Not that I really believed—Oh, Janet! You need help."

I felt my lower lip quiver, my chin knot.

"Give me the gun, Janet, do. It'll be all right. We'll get you into therapy—get you all the help you need."

25

" 'Help'!" Jack repeated. There was more than mere disgust in his voice. There was cold, concentrated hatred. "You think because you know every shrink and every judge in town, you're going to walk away from this, don't you, Janet? Beat the system like you do for the scum you represent." He took a step toward me, raising a clenched fist. "Well, you're *not!* Not if I have to—"

"Oh, Howie—listen to him. He deserves to die. He's been mean to me all along, for *years*—cheating on me, lying to me. He's *got* to pay for it."

"It's you I'm thinking of, Janet." Howie stepped between me and Jack, holding out his hand. He looked like a frightened deer. "For God's *sake.*" Howie, shrill? "For your own sake. Please. Give me the gun."

I could see Jack moving stealthily closer, using Howie for cover. I took a sideways step, trying to get a clear shot, but Howie ducked sideways, too, blocking my path.

Damn Howie! He was *my* associate, *my* friend—and he'd sided with Jack. Everyone sided with Jack.

Howie reached for the gun, Jack three paces behind him. Another second and they'd have me. Unless—

I'd won a couple of insanity acquittals; I knew what the shrinks looked for. And I was a good actress—as a trial lawyer, I had to be. With luck I could pull it off.

Two shots was all it took.

Destroying Angel

I was squatting a few feet from a live oak tree, poison oak all around me (an occupational hazard for mycologists). I brushed wet leaves off a small mound and found two young mushrooms. I carefully dug around one of them with my trowel, coaxing it out of the ground.

I held it up and looked at it. It was a perfect woodland agaricus. The cap was firm, snow white with a hint of yellow. The gills under the cap were still white, chocolate-colored spores hadn't yet tinged them. A ring of tissue, an annulus, circled the stipe like a floppy collar. A few strands of mycelia, the underground plant of which the mushroom is the fruit, hung from the base. I pinched the mycelia off and smelled the gills. The woodland agaricus smells like it tastes, like a cross between a mushroom, an apple, and a stalk of fennel.

I brushed leaves off the other mushroom and dug it out of the ground. It resembled the first mushroom. It had a white cap, white gills, an annulus. But a fleshy volva covered the bottom third of the stipe like a small paper bag. It was all that remained of a fungal "egg" from which stipe and cap had burst; characteristic of Amanitas, not Agaricus. The volva was the reason I'd dug so carefully around the base of the mushroom. I had to be sure I'd dug the whole thing out. If I'd left the volva in the ground, the mushroom would have been virtually indistinguishable from the woodland agaricus.

The mushroom was beautiful, pristine, stately, reputedly delicious (though you wouldn't live to eat it a second time).

But it was a deadly Amanita, a destroying angel, and I left it on the carpet of duff.

I filled my basket with woodland agaricus and I littered the duff with discarded destroying angels. A flock of birds swooped out of a tree and startled me off my haunches and onto my back, and I decided to call it a morning.

I walked the three or four miles back to the road, rubber boots squelching through mud. I watched mist float over manzanitas, drift along horizontal branches of live oaks, drip through mosses, mute the evergreen of firs and redwoods. The air smelled of loam and wet leaves and pine sap. Woodpeckers tapped, squirrels scrambled, and birds drank from curled bark. There were mushrooms everywhere, tiny brown ones no one had bothered to classify, fuchsia-colored Russolas, bits of orange chanterelles peeking out of leaf mounds. Most people don't see anything but leaves and pine needles when they look at a forest floor, they don't recognize the subtle patterns. But then, most people are content to see nature from a car window, to do their hiking in a shopping mall, to settle for flavorless mass-produced fungi.

Not me.

The museum was ready for the annual Fungus Fair. We'd carried the stuffed coyotes and pumas and the trays of butterflies and beetles down to the basement. We'd wheeled the waterfowl displays into the gift shop. There was still an occasional otter or egret peeking out from behind a table, but we'd managed to clear most of the main room.

We'd covered several tables with sand sculpted into gentle hills (two days' work), and we'd covered the sand with duff (another whole day). We had a hundred and twenty-seven species of fungus scattered over this ersatz forest floor, all labeled with Latin and common names and descriptions of their properties. Some were edible, some were medicinal, some glowed in the dark, some bled colored latex, some were used to make dye, some were used to make rocket fuel, some were poisonous. All were fascinating. To me, anyway. But then, I write mushroom field guides. I teach mushroom identification classes.

"Looks good." James Ransome, the museum curator, glowed with satisfaction. James has a square pink face, rimless aviator glasses, and wavy black hair. He's fortyish with a little potbelly under his inevitable button-down shirt and sweater vest. I like James a lot.

"We should move the knobcone pines," Don Herlihy grumbled. Again.

Don was doing me a favor, helping out with the fair. He helps every year. He's a botanist and an ornithologist; like me, not affiliated with a university. He gets by landscaping, specializing in drought-resistant native plants. He's a friend from a dozen college botany labs, and he throws a little landscaping my way when he's got the extra work and my museum classes aren't paying the rent. I wish Don were more than just a friend, but he always goes for the angora-sweater type. I keep hoping.

"They're going to fry when the sun shifts." Don didn't think we should bring in potted trees at all, but James wanted "atmosphere," and it was James's museum.

I didn't care much about atmosphere, but I cared less about the knobcones. I just wanted peace between my two best friends.

I said, "You know what I found this morning?"

Don continued scowling at the scraggly pines. "They'll get knocked over—if they don't fry first."

"We need them to screen the tidepool tank." James was calm, knowing he'd get his way, as usual. "Last year, we found it full of Dixie cups and plastic forks." 🎗

"Woodland agaricus," I continued. "I'm going to sauté it this afternoon as part of the tasting."

James blinked at me. "You cooked that for me a few years ago. Told me never to harvest it alone."

"It's easy to mistake for destroying angels." I bent over my basket of agaricus, pulling out a young specimen. "But that's the beauty of it. Very few people have the expertise to harvest it." I glanced at a table set up with hot plates and frying pans for the mushroom tasting. "People coming today probably won't ever get to taste it again."

James took the agaricus from me, turning it over. He knew enough about mushrooms to spot differences and appreciate similarities—if someone else made the initial identification.

Don walked over to the row of spindly pines, pulling them a few inches farther from the window. He always sweated the small stuff—and looked at me like I should back him up. When I didn't, he scowled. "Even experts make mistakes, Lucy."

James didn't bother moving the trees back. Later, I knew, we'd find them where he wanted them.

Don scratched his thick beard, squinting at me like I'd wimped out on him. "Guy who taught me everything I know about rock climbing fell and broke his neck in the Tetons last summer."

"Thanks for the vote of confidence." I took the agaricus back from James. "In the history of mycology, no expert—I don't mean guys who take a class or two and go out with their field guides—no *professional* has ever died of mushroom poisoning." I could feel myself flush. People are so damn afraid of mushrooms. It's irrational, something you don't see in other cultures, where families routinely go mushroom hunting together. "Look, no one ever worries about their parsley being hemlock or their bay leaves being oleander. People don't get scared that whoever harvested it—

"Uh-oh," James said grimly. "Lucy's hobbyhorse."

There was a tapping sound from the front of the museum. Someone knocking on the glass doors. Probably several people. The Fungus Fair always attracts a big crowd: amateur naturalists, people with kids, hippie types into natural dyes and psychedelics, mushroom gourmets, people who just like a colorful display.

By the time I finished the yarn-dyeing demonstration and spent some time identifying mushrooms people had found in their lawns, there were maybe fifty people jammed into the main room.

Time to cook some mushrooms.

I started with shaggy parasols, went on to horns of plenty, chanterelles, the prince, coccoli, ceps. So different from each other, with flavors ranging brothy to herby to fruity, and so very different from that Velveeta of fungus, the supermarket mushroom..

It got pretty frantic: people trooping by with little Dixie cups and plastic forks, and always a couple of gourmets to tell you a better way to cook whatever you're cooking (as if you can go wrong sautéing in butter), and then every time James had the tiniest problem, he wanted me to leave everything and come solve it, so I ended up sweating and rushing around replacing maggoty mushrooms from baskets of extras in the basement, and getting more butter, and checking to see if the yarn from the dyeing demonstration was drying okay.

One thing I did make time to do: I bent down and looked through the basket of woodland agaricus. A couple of caps had snapped off their stipes, but that always happens when you transport mushrooms. No volvas on any of the stipes.

By the time I started frying the agaricus, the place was so

crowded, you could hardly move. I felt clammy from the buttery steam, tired from days of gathering and planning and getting the museum ready. It sort of hit me all at once, and I remember thinking as I sliced up the agaricus how glad I was I'd gone out to the woods that morning. The woods were a tonic, just to think about.

James's wife came in and interrupted my meditation. Karen Ransome was a voluptuous, big-eyed woman with fluffy yellow hair and a lot of wiggly, giggly mannerisms. I didn't know her very well, even though I hung out with James a lot. Mostly I heard about her from Mary Clardy, who runs the museum gift shop. Mary told me Karen didn't like to hike, and wasn't it too bad because James enjoyed it so much, and you'd think Karen could take the kids to their soccer games once in a while and let James have a free Saturday, and wasn't it awful that Karen expected James to watch the kids on weekends, considering she left them with baby-sitters all week long even though she didn't work for a living, and Karen must realize it didn't help James's career when she got drunk at Museum Committee parties and flirted with the city attorney.

Karen came and stood beside me while I cooked. She chattered about a shopping excursion, but I wasn't really listening to her. Her breath smelled of booze, and she laughed and said, "This isn't one of those mushrooms you can't eat if you've been drinking, is it?"

There's a kind of inky cap that turns your nose and fingers red and makes your heart pound wildly for a few hours if you consume it with alcohol.

I scooped some mushroom into a Dixie cup. "No. Here, be my guinea pig. Woodland agaricus."

James came out of the gift shop, saw Karen eating the agaricus, and turned a little red. He pushed across to us in time to hear Karen repeat, "Woodland 'garicus," and giggle.

James looked embarrassed. He usually did in public with his wife. He murmured, "Karen, where are the kids?"

She wrinkled up her nose. "Guess I better go relieve the sitter—boy next door, honey, with all the freckles, you know who I mean. Let me just go to the gift stop—gift *shop*—"

"No!" James looked alarmed. "He can't be ten yet. Go see what the kids—" He put his arm around her, marching her to the door. I heard him ask where had she *been,* anyway.

I thought maybe he should have called her a cab, but he was a better judge than I was.

People were lined up to taste the agaricus. I watched their faces as they tasted it. Many had never tasted wild mushrooms. They looked like they'd gone to heaven.

I decided to fry up a second panful when James came back. "Everyone loves it," I boasted.

James seemed distracted. He helped me wipe off a couple of caps, then worked his way through the crowd toward the gift shop.

A young couple, wrapped in woolly scarves and looking like refugees from Woodstock, stood beside the table, Dixie cups at the ready. The woman, long-haired with a vaguely foolish expression, was flipping through a pamphlet of mine they sell in the gift shop, titled "Edible Mushrooms and Their Nonedible Look-alikes." The young man, whose smile was irresistible, asked me what I was cooking, and I told him.

The woman pointed to a photograph of the woodland agaricus in my pamphlet. "This one? The one it says not to pick unless an expert says it's okay?"

"Well, she's an expert," the man pointed out. "We usually stick to fly agaric." He grinned. "No mistaking that."

The fly agaric is bright red with cottony white "warts" (actually bits of a burst veil). It's psychotropic. Used for thousands of years in places like Siberia where alcohol made a late appearance.

I tried not to look too disapproving, but I hate people who think of mushrooms as just another way to get high.

Mary Clardy materialized beside me, her porcelain cheeks flushed almost as red as her curls.

"I saw Karen leaving. 'A happy drunk.' " Mary's tone was sarcastic. "They always think that about themselves, don't they?" Her chin was thrust forward.

The scarf-wrapped couple was exclaiming about the woodland agaricus, but Mary had interposed herself between me and the compliments.

"It's been ridiculous around here lately," she complained, pulling furry puffs off her sweater. "James having to run out of meetings to pick up those kids. Someone should report Karen for child neglect."

Don Herlihy joined us, homing in on Mary's pheromones, damn him. He was supposed to be giving a demonstration on how nurseries coat sapling roots with spores. The mushroom mycelia provide a protective sheath for the roots. Trees grow twice as tall when they grow with mushrooms.

Mary turned to Don with a slightly smug smile, the angora queen and her courtier. "I hear you're leaving us," she said, putting some sadness into her voice. "Taking a job down south."

I turned off the hot plate, not looking at Don. We'd covered thousands of acres together looking for mushrooms, looking for night herons, looking for obscure strands of fescue for his botany masters. It was the closest I'd come to romance. He and James and the classes I taught were my entire social life.

Don shuffled a step closer to me, standing stiffly. His clothes smelled of damp grass. "I guess I'm getting old." He sounded guilty, hadn't even told me he was thinking of going. "The knee's bothering me more and more. And with the wet weather this year . . . The money . . ."

I knew he was just squeaking by, that's how it always is with us. But I guess I thought it didn't matter to him. I guess I depended on it not mattering. Because if it mattered to him, maybe it should matter to me. If Don Herlihy put on a suit, maybe I'd have to, too, someday soon.

James wandered back over, looking a little surprised to find the three of us—the help—huddled together, not identifying, demonstrating, or selling anything.

I glanced at Don and found him giving Mary a heart-on-his-sleeve kind of look.

Mary had the same look, but it was aimed at James.

I excused myself and dashed down to the basement. It was cool and dark down there, just me and the stuffed coyotes, the boxes of mushrooms, the mountains of leftover duff. I sat at the fungus-strewn conference table and I could almost see my students emptying their baskets, chattering about what they'd found in the woods, about the "one that got away," that inevitable boletus ("this big") that was riddled with maggots.

I was thirty-one years old and nobody loved me. I was too broke to afford a decent car, even secondhand. I was forever choosing between housemates or a hovel (just now, it was the hovel). I wore my clothes until the flannel turned to powder. But I had my classes, didn't I? I'd generated a lot of enthusiasm for fungus over the years, and I'd knocked down a lot of silly phobias. I was out in the woods most days. That should count for something, shouldn't it?

It should count for something with Don, bad knee or not. *I* should count for something.

The basement door swung open. "What I wish," Don said

from the doorway, "is that I had a rich wife, like James. In fact"—a gloomy frown—"I wish I *were* James. I wish I had a silver Audi and a big house. I wish I had a job where people did what I told them."

"James isn't happy," I replied, though I'd never considered the point before.

Don shrugged. "Mary's crazy about him because she can't have him." I knew the feeling. "Even his problems work to his advantage."

"Where are you going?"

"Electronics firm in Encino."

Encino. Endless, unshaded concrete.

Please, God, may I never end up in Encino.

The lab technician at Community Hospital handed me a box of glass slides. This made the third time in eight years I'd done them this service. The third time in eight years they'd suspected mushroom poisoning and summoned the local expert. But it was different this time. I heard the slides rattle as I took the box in hand.

I pulled out a slide and, with a sterile swab, smeared some brown matter over the center. It was from a petri dish labeled "Feces—Peterson, Robin J." I dropped a coverslip into place.

I knew I would find some spores. I knew it because I'd watched Robin Peterson eat mushrooms. I'd watched him taste my woodland agaricus and smile a charming smile and try to tell me how much he loved it (with Mary Clardy in the way).

I told them at the hospital, "I didn't make a mistake—honest! Peterson ate a harmless mushroom. If he's sick, it's some kind of one-in-a-million allergy. That's all."

But they said he was showing signs of liver damage. They worried about kidney failure. The kind of symptoms produced by amanita toxins. By the destroying angel.

I maneuvered the slide back and forth until I spotted two quivering spores in the miasma. One was brown and oval. The woodland agaricus has brown oval spores. The other was white and round. I sat back. It was an Amanita (not an Agaricus) spore.

All Amanitas have round, white spores, but not all Amanitas are poisonous. There were three, maybe four edible species fruiting in nearby woods and fields. I closed my eyes and envisioned them, trying to influence the spores on the slide. Maybe Peterson had gotten hold of one of the edibles. Maybe this wasn't a death sentence.

I reached for the tiny stoppered bottle I'd brought with me. It was full of Melzer's reagent, an oily, yellow-red iodine solution. It stains certain spores— "amyloid" spores—gray. The deadly Amanitas have amyloid spores. The edible Amanitas don't.

I put a drop of Melzer's at the edge of the coverslip and watched it seep into the broth, tinging the whole mess grenadine. I breathed deeply, hoped deeply, and looked into the microscope.

The spore had turned light gray. It was amyloid.

Robin Peterson was lying there with a bunch of tubes coming out of him and a computer monitor blipping beside his bed. His mouth was hanging open and his skin was a dull apricot color with bruises all over it. I was too shaken to ask him if he'd gone collecting on his own, if he'd found himself some Amanitas and made a meal of them.

The poor man began retching. A nurse peeled the sheet off his abdomen and legs, and I could see that he lay in a pool of bloody excrement. It was the most awful sight I'd ever seen. I backed out of Intensive Care. I backed into James.

James was talking to a doctor and the doctor was saying, "Judging by the extent of liver and kidney damage—I believe it's been sixteen hours since he ingested the fungus?"

"Usually it takes longer," I said mechanically. "As long as three days for symptoms to show up."

The doctor shook his head angrily. "And a small amount can be fatal?"

"Two cubic centimeters." My voice seemed disembodied, like something out of the PA system. "That's the smallest known fatal dose."

"One mushroom, in other words."

"Yes, but—"

"But nothing." The doctor rubbed liver-spotted knuckles over Peterson's chart, as if trying to erase it. "Your mushroom's going to kill this man if we don't find him a new liver pretty damn soon."

"I gave him a harmless Agaricus, a relative of the supermarket mushroom. I know my mushrooms. Honestly! I wouldn't have—I *didn't*—make a mistake."

James put his arm around me, wincing. "Of course not, Lucy. Of course he didn't get the mushroom from you. As soon as he can be asked, he'll tell them."

The doctor looked like it cost him a lot not to slap us. He pushed between us and went back into Intensive Care.

James pulled me onto a padded bench. There was a sheen to his pale skin. "Don't let this get to you, Lucy. You know this isn't your fault." He searched my eyes. "You *know* that." But it sounded like a question.

"What about the other people?"

He touched my cheek. "What other people?"

"Who had mushrooms at the Fair. They'll get scared when they hear."

He sighed, looking away. "The Museum Association and

the city attorney have insisted we broadcast an appeal, telling everyone who had mushrooms at the Fair to come to the hospital." He looked at me again. "But it's just to satisfy the lawyers. Don't take it as a vote of no confidence. People who know you aren't going to bother."

"We'll never be able to serve mushrooms again, will we?" Whatever happened to Robin Peterson, the Fungus Fair was dead. Such a good little fair too. And no one would want to take my classes anymore.

I felt selfish thinking about it, with Peterson in there passing blood.

A woman drifted out of the elevator toward us. Peterson's companion of the day before, with her lank, center-parted hair and layers of sixties clothes.

She stopped when she saw me. She bent close, close enough for me to smell patchouli and damp wool.

It was easier to focus on her scarf than her face, under the circumstances. "Jack-o-lantern mushrooms," I murmured.

She fingered the scarf. "Uh-huh. We boiled them and put in chrome and iron and alum to get these colors."

"You know about mushrooms."

She nodded.

"Did Peterson go collecting? Before the fair? Or after?"

"No." She startled me by stroking my hair. "But it's not your fault. It's Robin's karma. I'm not sick. You're not sick. It must be Robin's karma. He's a fisher. A tuna fisher."

"Are you sure he didn't go collecting?"

"We didn't go out. We had Soma at home, dried. We ate that." Her face crinkled, as if the memory disturbed her. "We saw dolphins, ones that drowned in Robin's nets."

Soma. The subject of a six-thousand-year-old treatise in the *Rg Vedas,* the oldest specimen of written language. Soma the ingestible god. Also known as *Amanita muscaria,* the fly agaric, psychotropic but "poisonous" only in the way alcohol and recreational drugs are poisonous. Its spores are not amyloid. It wasn't a fly agaric spore I'd found and stained on that glass slide.

The doctor came out and stood over us. "Peterson's dead."

James wrapped his arms around me. The young woman dropped to the floor, curling into an upright fetal position. "I can feel his soul," she whispered. Her head snapped back and she stared at me. "He'll speak to you in Soma."

James stayed with me that night, brewing me pots of herb tea that I couldn't drink and talking to me about anything, everything: his kids, his holidays, what we could expect from the wet weather in terms of timing the Wildflower Festival.

I knew that outside our cocoon, Fungus Fair attendees rushed themselves to the hospital; botanists who knew nothing about fungus fueled the public's phobia with misinformation; newspapers published alarmist lies. I'd spent a career trying to change people's attitudes about one of the world's most intriguing (and often health-preserving) life-forms. It was all wiped out now, all my work—seven six-session classes a year for eight years, the expeditions I'd led, two editions of my field guide, the edible mushrooms pamphlet. Now people would remember me as the mycologist who'd killed a man at a mushroom fair.

And I hadn't. How could I have made a mistake? I know mushrooms, really know them.

I felt like jumping off a cliff.

James tried hard to make me feel better, but I could see how upset he was, underneath. I ended up crying all over him.

I fell asleep around dawn, with James yawning and telling

me about a cruise to Alaska, a cruise he very much wanted to take if he could just persuade Karen to travel so far from Macy's.

I woke up a few hours later to find James asleep in my sprung easy chair. I tiptoed out of the house (maybe "shack" is a better word), put on my boots, and drove out to the woods. It's the only place I feel at home.

The mushrooms were beautiful, tomato-red with puffy white "warts." They were in a clearing by themselves, the center of attention, fresh and perfect, without a single bug in their gills, without a trace of decay. Yet I looked at them and felt afraid, afraid of what they might do to me. I reminded myself that people had been eating them for thousands of years. And I'd never heard of any fatalities (except in a British mystery novel).

I was doing it myself—letting phobia overcome what I knew to be true about the mushroom.

I forced myself to kneel in the duff before the great god Soma. At the base of one mushroom, a stunned fly skittered in the wind, attracted and then drugged by the fungus.

I snapped the broad caps off their stipes.

When I got home, James was gone. Just as well.

I sliced the fly agaric and spent an hour trying to copy the method of ingestion described by the Aryans in the *Rg Vedas*. I swallowed the yogurty mess. It tasted like moldy leaves.

For half an hour nothing happened, except that I was scared: scared of the mushroom and scared of Robin Peterson's ghost.

And then I was on the floor, supine and sweating. The ceiling swirled. For years I'd studied mushrooms, hunted them, examined them under microscopes, cooked them, served them, eaten them, arranged them, lectured about them, and photographed them. Now I saw myself as part of a continuum. I saw reindeer butt each other in savage contest for the fungus, I saw Aryan priests drink Soma milk, I saw bearded Siberians leap and stagger and laugh, I saw flower children peel the red skin off the cap and roll it into cigarettes.

And then I saw myself:

A cool, misty morning, me with my raincoat on, my basket on the ground beside me. There were two dozen mushrooms in it already, some very young with veils covering their white gills, some with broad caps and gills dusted with brown spores.

I looked up. The wet branches of a live oak spread like gnarled arms against the white of the sky. Birds chattered somewhere in the tree, calling *scree scree scree*.

I looked back down. There were several mushrooms on the duff. Destroying angels, their caps so similar to the woodland agaricus that only the sacklike volva at the base of the stipe proclaimed them to be deadly.

I looked at the mushrooms in my basket. I inhaled the cold air. I listened to the *scree* of birds overhead, to the rustling of squirrels and the distant thud of falling pinecones. Life was good.

I dug in the duff. There were two young mushrooms there, caps snow white, round and small with partial veils and strong, crisp stipes. I dug carefully, recognizing the danger.

One was a destroying angel and one was a woodland agaricus. Strands of mycelia hung from the base of one, and I pinched them off. The other was covered with a sacklike volva. I tossed that mushroom. Tossed it and then noticed a purple stain on its volva, like a bit of oozy ink.

It wasn't uncommon to find an aberrant mushroom, a mushroom harboring some unusual parasite or staining some uncharacteristic shade. I enjoyed finding the aberrations, they were part of the fun of hunting.

I picked up the destroying angel and sloughed off the stained volva. The ooze had not touched the stipe. Probably something in the ground, nothing to do with the mushroom itself. I tossed it aside again.

From the branches overhead, the *scree scree scree* of birds grew frantic. I looked up in time to see a small cloud of them swooping down. They seemed to be diving for me. I fell out of my squat and onto my back. As the birds pulled up and flew away, I saw a flash of white under their wings. I'd have to ask Don what kind they were.

I stood up, pulling twigs out of my hair and flicking soggy duff off my raincoat.

I bent to pick up my basket. Time to go to the museum.

I reached out to pick up the young woodland agaricus I'd just found.

Robin Peterson's icy hand closed over mine as I picked up the wrong mushroom.

A pounding on my front door dragged me out of a stuporous sleep. Someone was shouting my name.

I sat up. My furniture was all rearranged, pulled to the middle of the room. Why the hell had I done that?

I crawled on hands and knees to the front door, using the knob to pull myself to my feet.

It was Don Herlihy. He looked ashen, ill. He said, "Did you hear about Karen yet? Karen Ransome?"

"Oh, my God." I'd handed James's wife a Dixie cup of what I thought was woodland agaricus. Handed it to her with a boastful word and a proud smile.

"She's dead, Lucy. James was away, I guess, for most of the night. And no one told Karen about going to the hospital to get tested. By the time James got home and found her, she was too far gone."

"James was over here," I heard myself say. "It's my fault Karen didn't get help in time."

Don said, "No, Lucy," but he didn't come in.

There was a receipt sticking out of his shirt pocket. I could see Community Hospital's logo. He'd been to the hospital to get tested. I had no right to feel hurt, but I did.

"Come in, Lucy," James said kindly. "I've been worrying about you."

I heard children crying somewhere in the upstairs of James's house, and I heard the calm voice of an adult woman. James wore jeans and cashmere. His skin looked like candle wax, he was so pale. His hair stood up in rumpled waves against a backdrop of oak paneling.

I followed him inside. I followed him through the living room, through the formal dining room, through the hall, and back into a kitchen bigger than my whole house. There was a sweater slung across the tile counter. Mary Clardy's. It was her voice I'd heard, her voice consoling the children.

"I'm most comfortable in this room," James said, running a listless hand over the tile. "In fact, it probably seems gruesome, but now that everyone's finally gone, I was going to chop some stuff for stir-fry."

"If it relaxes you." How many times had I watched James slice mushrooms and debone chicken? My friend, how kind of him to let me into his kitchen.

"It's awful, but I'm hungry. I just—" He looked at me with bright eyes. "Have a meal with me, would you, Lucy? Make me feel like I'm not being abnormal?"

I couldn't imagine forcing food down my throat. "If you want me to. If you're really not—" Not mad at me.

He turned and began collecting things: A wok, some ginger, calamari in a plastic bag, oyster mushrooms, supermarket agaricus, bok choy, sesame oil.

I watched him set up the wok, heat the oil, toss in the ginger, then the bok choy. What I saw was my own hand reaching out for that one fatal mushroom, the one on the duff.

Such a small mushroom, such a small destroying angel to kill two healthy—

It was like a knife in my gut: A small mushroom. A very small mushroom to have killed two healthy people.

The smallest fatal dose on record was two cubic centimeters, the size of a modest cap.

I watched James slice the oyster mushrooms and the supermarket mushrooms. And I remembered him wiping a cap and handing it to me at the Fungus Fair. I'd been slicing woodland agaricus into the skillet, right before serving Robin Peterson. Right *after* serving Karen Ransome.

James looked at me, his head cocked. Sighing, he tossed handful of sliced mushrooms into the wok.

He could have it all now. Karen's wealth. Mary's love.

From that perspective, it was convenient he'd spent the night supporting and consoling me. Convenient he didn't tell his wife to watch for signs of mushroom poisoning, that he wasn't home to notice her symptoms and rush her to the hospital.

I watched James reach into a cupboard and pull out two dishes and two wineglasses. He handed the glasses to me.

We'd done this many times over the last eight years. I'd set the breakfast-nook table a hundred times. A hundred times we'd discussed museum business over stir-fry or bagels or mulligatawny soup, with Karen passed out drunk upstairs.

I pulled place mats out of a hutch, pulled a bottle of Chardonnay off the wine rack, pulled chopsticks out of the drawer. My back was to James. I was afraid—horrified by the suspicion I suddenly harbored.

He brought two steaming bowls of stir-fry to the table. He set one at my usual place. "No oyster sauce in that one," he said. "I know you hate the stuff."

I know how much destroying angel it takes to kill two people. I know that if I did make a mistake, it involved only one mushroom, the one with the stained volva. I know that if I did make a mistake, only one person would be dead now, not two.

I picked up my chopsticks and glanced down at the bowl. Sesame oil sizzled on a bed of mushrooms, calamari, and vegetables.

I unfolded my linen napkin while James uncorked the wine.

I looked around the room. The wainscoting was golden oak, the walls were papered a rich green, the floor was tiled in glossy terra-cotta. The breakfast nook windows faced a koi pond ringed with willows.

I remembered Don Herlihy saying, "I wish I had a rich wife."

And I was suddenly sure: I did not see the spirit of Robin Peterson in my psychotropic vision. I did not see the truth, I saw my own fear. My worst nightmare.

I would not have picked up the wrong mushroom. Even if I had, I'd have noticed *something,* something a little odd about the sloughed stipe when I examined the mushrooms later.

It wasn't my mistake. Relief momentarily blurred my vision, like film melting in a projector.

Then I focused on James.

James. He had watched Karen eat the woodland agaricus. She'd been drinking again, neglecting the children. So unlike Mary Clardy.

He would serve Karen destroying angels at home, later. He would be rid of her. He would rescue his children from her incompetent care without depriving them of her big house. And it would look like an accident. An honest mistake. Especially if someone else at the fair got sick too.

After Karen left the museum, James handed me a mushroom cap to slice and serve. A destroying angel from the museum display. He would not have known so small a quantity could kill. Two cubic centimeters—only a mushroom expert would know that.

Now James said, "Eat it while it's hot, Lucy. There's comfort in food." He attacked his stir-fry like he needed comfort badly.

But he was doing better than me. He had a big house and two nice kids and somebody to love him. What did I have?

I used to think I had two friends, maybe not much else, but two best friends.

Don Herlihy, and he was leaving.

And James Ransome. How many canoe trips had we taken together? How many exhibits had we set up?

I thought James cared about me. How could he ruin my reputation—my *life*—just to arrange things so they suited him better?

I poked at the contents of my bowl.

Even if I told people, they wouldn't believe me. They'd consider it a rank excuse, a cheap shot, an attempt to pass the buck. And I couldn't prove anything anyway. Even if I wanted to orphan James's kids, I couldn't prove anything.

Two best friends. I thought of Don Herlihy shuffling on my doorstep, that hospital receipt in his pocket. After years of studying with him, working with him, he didn't trust me. He didn't love me.

And James. I thought he was my friend, staying with me

last night. But he'd wrecked my life.

No matter what I did or said now, my career was ruined. No one would believe it wasn't my fault. If I couldn't convince Don Herlihy, how could I convince a bunch of strangers?

I'd never be considered an "expert" again, only someone who, in her hubris, continued denying what everybody else knew: that mushrooms should be feared and shunned, regardless of who serves them.

James was slumped over his meal now, not eating. His eyelids looked painfully puffy and red.

I was surprised I didn't feel more anger. Maybe I was too sad. Maybe I couldn't stand to let go of my last friend.

I tasted a few slivers of mushroom. They were perfectly seasoned. James was a good cook. Mary was lucky.

Upstairs somewhere, children's voices were raised with Mary's in a hymn. James covered his eyes with his hands.

No, it wouldn't do me any good to accuse James. Proof required confidence in my expertise. No one would believe me and no one would trust me, ever again. I'd never earn a living as a mycologist, ever again. I would have to put on a suit. Work in some concrete purgatory.

I couldn't live with it. It was as simple as that: I couldn't live with it.

Today I had experimented with Soma, something I never thought that I would do. Tonight I would experiment again. I would go home and eat the destroying angel. I would see if it really was delicious.

Easy Go

I kept my eyes on the sidewalk, on river patterns of sticky urine congealing in the morning sun, catching pigeon feathers. Around me old men scratched and coughed and slid up walls they'd hugged for shelter in the night. Now and then, a briefcase darted by, a pair of shined shoes hurried toward City Hall, toward the Federal Building, toward the State Court of Appeal. I kept my eyes lowered. I knew too many lawyers in San Francisco, and they knew too much about me.

The offices of the State Bar of California are just a few blocks from the heart of San Francisco's Tenderloin. And the Tenderloin does have a heart: for the thousands of teenage prostitutes of both sexes, for the rummies and runaways and addicts at peep shows, there is at least a soup kitchen, at least a church with gaudily uplifting angels. But try to find the State Bar's heart. It doesn't have one, just a ledger.

I climbed the steps. I should have been glad to climb them; I'd waited three years to do it. Three years plus one day since they'd cut off my buttons and epaulets. Three years of paying an "inactive status" fee (and galling it had been, believe me). Now, for an additional four hundred and thirty dollars and proof I'd retaken the professional responsibility exam, I would once again receive a flimsy paper card with perforated edges. Frances Valentine, it would read, Active Member, State Bar of California.

The State Bar. After my disciplinary proceeding, a tragic-faced girl stopped me in the hall to say that the State Bar was hiring. You don't need anything but a law degree to work there, it didn't matter that my license had been suspended. I'd bitten my lip to refrain from telling her I'd rather empty bedpans. She didn't deserve the splash of acid that had grown to replace pleasantries in my conversational style.

I didn't empty bedpans. I took a bus to a hot griddle of a town with too many Burger Kings. I bought a newspaper and found a job in a title company with a tiled roof. That was the first of six white collar jobs I took in different valley towns, most of them with a Denny's and a Woolworth's and not much else.

I could have done it differently, could have gone to some little gem of a seacoast town, maybe worked as a paralegal, maybe taught in some small college. I could have done myself and my resume that favor.

But I wanted Bradley Allen Palmer to know he'd ruined me. I wasn't sure he cared, but I wanted him to know.

My Persian carpet was soiled and stained after three years of rough treatment by the woman to whom I'd sublet my apartment. The afternoon light showed water spots and gouges on the dusty oak desk and table. Fleas hopped on the sofa, searching frantically for the cat I'd evicted.

I opened the bay windows, grateful that my Chinese neighbors still cultivated small flowering trees, still hung vegetables to dry like laundry, still maintained their tiny fish pond. The twin spires of St. Ignatius, blurry with fog, hovered over distant rooftops. Damp wind rustled the want ads spread out on my desk, want ads from both San Francisco papers, from the Oakland paper, from the *Advocate Journal*, from *California Lawyer*.

I'd crossed out a few ads: sole practitioners who couldn't afford to be fussy, couldn't afford to worry about a little moral turpitude in their employees' past—maybe even had a little in their own. Men paying seventeen, eighteen thousand in a town where forty is considered low. But they all knew my story, let me know there were thousands of virgin lawyers out there. One expressed amazement that I hadn't been disbarred. A distinction without a difference, if no one would hire me.

I'd had my resume redone. Three-quarters of the page listed my honors in painful detail: top five percent; law review; student article published; clerk for the Honorable Steven K. Dresge; another article published; teacher of legal writing at a downtown law school; associate with Winship, McAuliffe, Potter & Tsieh, one of the better criminal law firms. Then a paragraph headed "Subsequent Employment" condensed the last three years of my life into categories: escrow clerk, loan officer's assistant, registrar's aide, junior budget analyst. At the bottom of the page, because honesty required it, I had written, "License to practice before the California Bar reinstated" and the date.

I felt a wrench of nausea—rent due soon and not much money in the bank. I remembered the hurry-up anxiety of a waiting time clock, deadening days of shuffling preprinted forms. Maybe the new resume was an exercise in false hope. All recredentialed and no place to go.

Bradley Palmer had made partner by now, pulling down a salary of $150,000 and a partnership share of that much or more. He'd taken me to Chez Panisse the night Millet, Wray & Weissel hired him, a three-hundred-dollar dinner for two, six years ago.

The last time I'd made love to Brad, it had been a foregone conclusion that we'd marry. We'd been in my apartment. This room had smelled of blossoms from the Chinese couple's trees. Now there was a faint zoo smell in the air from cat puddles sunbaked into the carpet.

Brad Palmer had prospered while I sweltered in secretarial-beige cubicles, spurning consolation. It wasn't *his* nose I'd cut off to spite my face.

If I closed my eyes, I could see Brad on top of me, his chest damp and hirsute, his arms tensed to support his weight, his wide-set eyes half closed, a vein standing out on his broad forehead, sweat beading on his flat cheeks, his thin lips parted, honey-colored hair damp at the hairline, stiffly combed back by my own fingers.

But then, I could also see him sitting in the State Bar hearing room, straight and handsome in his banker's blue suit. testifying against me.

I rode the elevator to the twenty-first floor of the financial district monolith. I walked into the offices of Millet, Wray & Weissel and handed their aristocratic, carefully painted receptionist my resume.

The woman took it, thanking me dismissively. "Will you make sure Bradley Palmer gets it?"

It was halfway to the "in" basket. Sighing, she diverted it to the blotter and scribbled "Attn: BAP" in the top corner. Then she glanced at the typeset name beneath her scrawl. Pencil arrested, she looked at me with startled interest. "Frances Valentine?"

I fought an impulse to deny it. "Yes."

"If you'll be seated a moment." She pressed a buzzer on her space-age telephone, mumbling something to someone.

Two minutes later, Brad stepped into the reception area.

He wore navy pin-striped wool, a white shirt, a maroon tie. His hairline had receded slightly. He sported a coppery new mustache that disguised the thinness of his lips and lent his face an air of reserved goodwill. His eyes were brighter blue than I remembered, his brows thicker, nose straighter, face bigger, shoulders wider. He even seemed taller.

I'd had three years to think about him. I'd experienced every shade of emotion, from crazy fury to tender regret, thinking about him. But I hadn't quite realized until yesterday, crying over want ads, that I didn't love him anymore. There was nothing left to fuel the rage.

There seemed to be several of me rising simultaneously to greet him. I shook his hand because the receptionist seemed to expect it of me.

She handed Brad my resume.

It took me a minute to find my voice. Three years is a long silence to break. "Do you need a law clerk? Or a paralegal?"

His eyes strayed to the bottom of the page to see how I'd handled my disgrace. A bit of color crept into his cheeks.

He murmured, "This way." As he led me down a suede-walled corridor, he kept glancing back, making sure (or maybe fearing) that I followed.

He preceded me into his office.

I walked around the room, looking at the plush wheat carpeting, the natural suede walls, the golden oak desk, the sienna leather chairs, the unglazed pottery, the Georgia O'Keeffe on a pine easel.

Brad watched me, a vein standing out on his forehead, his eyes bright. "I need some kind of transition on my resume, Brad. I want to practice law again."

"Why here?"

"No one else will hire me." *And maybe you think you owe me a favor.*

"Frannie, it would be a hard sell. To say the least."

I visualized him in front of the hiring committee. How would he explain what I'd done? Baldly perhaps: You see, colleagues, Ms. Valentine was convinced her client would be killed in prison. So she tried to buy him a forged passport. She contacted the passport forger herself. She then told her fiancé (maybe Brad would let the word hang in the air) what she'd done. Her fiancé was sure she'd get caught if she followed through. Her fiancé thought she'd gone a little crazy, maybe even thought she was a little in love with her handsome client. With characteristic paternalism, her fiancé contacted the State Bar to keep her out of worse trouble. (Or maybe he was jealous and angry. Who could tell, with his lawyer face wiped clean of emotion?)

Her fiancé didn't care if her client was blinded and carved up with sharpened spoons. Didn't care if he lay in a pool of blood for hours while the prison guard ignored him. Didn't care if it took him four slow days to die. Said she was lucky he'd died, in fact. Lucky because the government was too embarrassed to indict her. Lucky because it remained a State Bar matter.

Lucky. Even Brad's facial flaws, the tired lines and receding hairline, were signs of success.

"Plus . . ." Brad remained poker-faced, straight-spined. "I don't want to be a target of recriminations. If I go to bat for you, I'll want some assurance that you don't blame me, that you've accepted the consequences of your actions."

I turned to the wall of windows on my right, stood there feeling like Kirk at the helm of the *Enterprise*. The detail was magnificent: furbelows and banners and awnings, Peter Max colors in plate-glass reflections, churches and Victorians hoisted to eye level by distant hills, buckets of cut flowers polka-dotting corners, bobbing streams of pedestrians, a brick plaza and its windblown fountain, the slow, noisy jerk of traffic. More to see in Brad's window than in entire inland valleys.

"The thing is, Brad, Raul Alegria accepted the consequences of your actions."

"You'd have been prosecuted if you'd gone any further." His voice seemed a dead and distant thing, the sentence three years stale.

"That was my risk to take. Or it should have been."

I heard the sigh of leather cushions, the creak of a swivel chair. "What do you want from me, Fran? I don't hear from you for three years. Like I'm the fucking bad guy. For keeping you out of jail. So? What do you want from me now?"

I considered leaving. But I'd already thrown away three years. Three years of flat horizon, static air, cloudless blue-white sky, like being trapped in a vast stoppered jar. What the hell had I proved? That I could make myself suffer?

I turned to face him. His arms were folded across his chest, his chin tucked down. Guarded.

I didn't love him anymore. Such a relief.

"No one will hire me," I said carefully. "You know how I feel about my work."

"Come on—how good's it going to look, a year or two here as a glorified law clerk?"

"Look where I am now. Look at my resume."

He scowled at his desktop. He was motionless at first, then he nodded slightly.

"Most places, I can't even get interviews. Even fly-by-night lawyers won't touch me." *And nobody in town owes me a favor; nobody but you.*

"Okay, Frannie." The new mustache hid the pained twitch of muscle at the corner of his mouth. I saw it in the paralyzed misery of his cheeks. I knew the face so well. "I'll square it somehow. Come in Monday."

I told myself it was the smartest thing I'd done in a long time. I told myself I was nothing but a whore. Probably both were true.

★ ★ ★ ★ ★

It was law clerk's work, writing up the results of my research so someone else could go into court and argue the actual motions. But that was okay.

The job wasn't as exciting as my old job at Winship, McAuliffe. But after three years of invisibility, that's not what I compared it with.

At the end of the second week, John V. Cusinich, a senior partner with coke-bottle glasses, a thin, pinch-lipped face, and slicked-back hair, came into my office. I was surprised. Cusinich was being considered for a federal court judgeship, adding much to his already considerable consequence. Until that morning, he'd barely deigned to nod to me. "You did this memo?" His magnified eyes examined the small, unadorned room with distaste.

"Yes. Is there some problem with it?"

"No. It's excellent. I didn't think we had any basis for our claim, but this is a very clever argument." He very nearly smiled, I think. "Good use of case law. I understand you have more experience than our other—than our clerks."

"I passed the bar six years ago. Clerked for the Northern District—Judge Dresge—and then spent two years at Winship, McAuliffe, Potter and Tsieh."

"Bradley mentioned that. Criminal law background. Actually,"—he brushed imaginary lint from his sleeve—"I talked to Roland Tsieh about you this morning. We've been asked to take on a criminal matter as a favor to a corporate client. You should look at the file. See what you think."

I already knew what I thought. The firm should take the case and let me handle it.

Watching Cusinich inspect my undecorated burlap walls, I felt light-headed, realized I was holding my breath.

That afternoon, a large abstract oil painting was removed

from above the Xerox machine and brought to my office. A man identifying himself as "maintenance" asked me where I wanted it. I didn't particularly like the splashes of ocher, tan, and pink, but I knew a vote of confidence when I saw it. I had the man hang it above my desk where it was clearly visible from the door.

The next day, Brad brought me a file folder. He glanced at the painting. "John Cusinich suggested I assign you this case."

"Is it the criminal matter he mentioned?"

"Yes."

I flipped the file open. A few notes on a phone conversation: client busted for growing marijuana in the Santa Cruz Mountains. No mention of when or how much. I'd need details, and I'd need them soon. "This office doesn't usually handle criminal cases, does it?"

"This is the only one. The defendant's father owns a brussels sprouts farm down the coast. We handle all his business affairs. That's why the son thought of us. We did tell him a criminal law firm might do a better job. But I guess he really wanted us. Asked John Cusinich if we had anybody here with criminal defense experience. I told John about you."

"I want the arrest report, indictment, all that stuff. Meet the client. Check out the scene."

A hesitant shuffle.

"I'm sure you know"—trying not to take the hesitation personally—"that it's a quick deadline for Motions to Suppress Evidence. Most of these cases are won or lost on that motion. I'm not trying to shirk my other work, but I need to move—"

"I'm just wondering . . ."

I looked up at him. "I remember how, Brad. Believe me."

"Okay."

With a parting glance at the oil painting, he left me to my first case in over three years.

When the client phoned Cusinich back, Cusinich put him through to me. His file was significantly thicker by then. I had an arrest report from the Santa Cruz County Sheriff's office, an indictment from the DA, and a Motion to Suppress Evidence well under way.

The client gave me directions to the mountain property from which police had seized twenty-six marijuana plants.

I drove down the coast, trying to enjoy the scenery. It was a clear breezy day, the sky streaked with clouds, the air fresh and salty. Men in straw cowboy hats bent over rows of greenery between the highway and the ocean cliffs. Some of the farmworkers were gathered around a pickup truck just off the road. Most were Hispanic men, short with broad chests and dusty clothes.

When I'd heard about Raul Alegria, I'd driven to a coastal farm and found Raul's mother in the middle of a field, sobbing and being comforted by men who looked like these men. I'd driven her to Folsom Prison, to the infirmary there. The drive had taken four hours, more or less, and Martina Alegria, a strong-looking woman with rough hands, had spent most of that time telling me what a good baby Raul had been, how he'd wanted to nurse all the time and been bigger than the other farmworkers' children.

I'd seen Martina Alegria again when I'd moved to Fairfield. She'd been picking lettuce and had a raw-looking pesticide rash on both arms. She'd come to the title company to bring me a plate of fried cookies and an icon of the Madonna. She'd cried a little and promised to buy a Mass for me next time she burned a candle for Raul. I hope she remembered.

About three-quarters of the way down to Santa Cruz, I

turned left, heading up Ben Lomond Mountain.

Half an hour later, I approached a rustic, plank-sided A-frame.

A man paced the road beside the driveway, running his hand over a lank mane of black hair. He motioned me to pull over, then helped me out of the car, murmuring, "Jerry Riener. Hi."

He might have been six four if he'd stood straight. He had puffy-lidded eyes and a square, stubbled jaw. He looked pale, maybe sick, maybe hung over. In top form, he'd have been male-model handsome, but he was far from top form. He wore a quilted jacket, patched and stained, shiny jeans and muddy boots.

For a second, he gaped at me in my city-slicker clothes. Then he said, "Oh man, I hope you can keep me out of jail. They'll kill me in there."

I felt sick. Something Brad had coached him to say? "Why would they do that—whoever 'they' are?"

He reeled slightly, as if my scorn had physical mass. "Don't you know what I used to do for a living?".

"No." I stuffed my hands into my jacket pockets. It was sunless and gloomy under the canopy of pines and redwoods. The air smelled musty and fungusy, of damp roots and rotting leaves.

Reiner's eyes narrowed. Suspicion? Displeasure? "I thought I—" He sighed heavily. "You mind a short hike? I'll take you where they harvested the pot."

We crossed the road, heading away from the house. The woods ended almost immediately, and we walked uphill onto acres of tumbling meadowland, knee-high in swaying grasses. Miles away, at the foot of the mountain, the sea glimmered, flecked with whitecaps.

Reiner inhaled deeply. "Botanically, it's very rich. Seventy percent of the plants in Thomas's *Flora of California* are in these mountains." He uprooted a pad-shaped bit of greenery. "Miners' lettuce. Edible." He squatted in the tall grass, shading his eyes as he looked up at me. "I've learned what's edible and what isn't in the last few years."

"What did you used to do for a living?"

"Prison guard. Soledad, among other places."

A prison guard. I thought of the guard who'd let Raul lie there half a morning bleeding. Folsom Prison had fired him, but no other action had been taken. He'd vanished before I had a chance to spit in his eye. Scot-free.

I heard myself murmur, "Do you know David Williams?"

Reiner shook his head. "Should I?"

"He was a guard at Folsom . . . Never mind." I felt a needling of irritation. New case, new start. Forget Raul. "Go on with what you were saying."

"Well, it's not a very popular profession." A hint of rueful grin, then, "The way you're looking at me—you know, somebody's got to do it. There's some hard, nasty folks in there and we can't *all* rely on someone else to watch them."

He stood, eyes flashing with defensive anger. Or maybe just fear. Soledad was a big place. No matter what jail Reiner ended up in—if he ended up in one—there would be a former Soledad inmate coming through, eventually.

"If someone did recognize you, what would he tell the other inmates about you?"

He stroked his jaw. "A diplomatic way of asking if I'm a sadistic asshole?"

"Are you?" My tone was sharp. Almost unprofessional.

"Goddamn." A stillborn grin. "Lady, who do you think is in there? Christian martyrs? We're talking serious gangs—people who literally bite each other's fingers off, ears off. Not nice people."

My first case in three years. Had I forgotten how to act professional? "I'm asking how they saw you, not how you saw them."

An exasperated wave of the arm. "I wasn't any rougher than I had to be. Maybe they thought I was an asshole at times. Sometimes you have to clamp down for their own protection." He looked suddenly weary. "It can be a real horror show, you have no idea. You start taking shit and there's no end to it. On the other hand, get too much in the middle and you get hurt big-time. To some extent, you leave it alone. Other times, you get heavy. It's a very fine line."

A screwed-up system, my old boss used to say. Accept that or find some other kind of law to practice.

"Tell me about your arrest."

Reiner brushed a lock of hair off his forehead. His hand was callused, nails trimmed but rough. His hand was shaking.

"It seems from your arrest report that the state has a very strong case against you, Mr. Reiner. If you are guilty . . ." Playing harbinger, my former boss called it; part of the job. "It might be possible to bargain the charge down to simple possession, if you're willing to plead guilty. It could mean a much shorter sentence. And something else you should consider: There's a statute allowing the government to confiscate your land if you're convicted of cultivating marijuana on it."

Jerry Reiner folded his arms over his chest. His eyes were open wide, unblinking. He looked like a wax statue.

I expected him to rail at the unfairness of the statute, the unfairness of the system. Most clients would. He didn't.

It was a minute, maybe longer, before he spoke. His lips moved without sound, at first. His color flooded back. Fight, not flight. "Look, I mean it, they'll kill me in there. So I'll just have to take my chances, okay?"

My mouth felt dry, my throat tight. Three years of bitter

nostalgia for criminal practice, but I'd let myself forget this part of it. Let myself forget how it felt to share a client's fear. Except Raul's.

Raul had said to me, "I won't last a week in there, Frances." And I'd replied, "Tell me what to do, and I'll do it."

To Jerry Reiner I said, "It's your decision, not mine."

His lips pursed and his brows pinched. There was determination in his eyes, raw and reckless. But no hint of supplication. No favors asked.

"So you won't buy me a fake passport?"

The air temperature seemed to drop twenty degrees. I felt myself take a slow step backward.

"I kept track of you after the State Bar gave you that little slap on the wrist!"

"How did you know about—"

"Alegria was scum. A punk. A snitch."

The landscape seemed to tilt. "How did you know Raul?"

He pointed at me, two quick stabs of the index finger. "I think it's bullshit you're at a fancy law firm now. What's the point of getting disbarred if you can go to work for a fancy law firm?"

"Why do you know this? Why do you care?"

"It's not right." Somewhere between a whine and a shout.

"Are you Jerry Reiner?"

"No." He shook his head widely, emphatically. "Never heard of him, except what I read in the paper about his arrest. The article said his father's a big-time farmer. I don't know what made me run down who the father's lawyer is. It was just a feeling I had, that he was your firm's client. It was just"—he kissed his fingertips—"karma."

I scanned the meadow. It ended in a tangle of shrubs. Then more forest.

"Who are you?"

"A three-year suspension—a fucking slap on the wrist! Now you're back at a fancy law firm."

"As a law clerk."

"You know what I've been doing for the last three years? Grunt fucking labor. When I can get it."

"David Williams. You're David Williams." You let Raul die. Let him lie in his own blood for hours.

He nodded. His eyes glinted, maybe with tears.

"It doesn't matter." I was chilled to the marrow in my wool suit. "Doesn't matter what happened to me." God knows I suffered as much as I could make myself suffer. "That's not the point. What about Raul? How could you leave him lying there?"

"I told you! Sometimes you can't get in the middle. You've got to let them put the message out: Here's what happens to guys try to rat out their friends and make a deal."

"Our system's based on making deals. If you can't protect a prisoner who's testified—"

" 'You.' If 'you' can't." He ran both hands over his hair. "Leave it up to the prison guards, the garbage collectors. Sure, shun them, act like they must be mean stupid sons of bitches to want to do the job, but leave it to them to keep the psychos chilled. 'You'! You have any idea what kind of powder keg it is? How rigid the codes are? Fuck. Sure, I could have jumped in the middle when they went for Alegria, maybe started a fucking riot, lots of gunfire and stabbing and maybe hostages and people dying, because that's the kind of place Folsom is. I could have rushed Alegria to the infirmary, but you know and I know he wouldn't have lasted an hour longer. Or even if he'd made it, they'd have got him next time, no joke."

There were times, living in Fairfield, in Woodland, that I'd stared at the flat line of sky on field and become overpowered by a sense of unreality. I'd attributed it to the sensory deprivation of a barren landscape.

But now, with grasses tickling my ankles and distant sea sparkling in my peripheral vision, I felt the same disconnection. Raul was dead. The man who'd let it happen shouted at me. Defending himself. As if I could ever forgive him.

"And then a bunch of fat bureaucrats sit in judgment— why didn't you stop it, all that bullshit. But if you're not there, you don't know. You can't know."

"I heard you got fired."

"Fucking right." He took two angry steps toward me, his face flushed red. "And what else am I trained for? Odd jobs, farm labor— I've been living in a Volkswagen squareback for three years, you know that? You know how hard it is to get by, get enough food when you're trying to save for rent? Find any kind of decent job—never mind meet women—when you're living out of a car?"

What was it Brad had said? Accept the consequences of your actions?

"Why?" I wondered. "Why did you go to all this trouble? Why lie about who you are? Why not just call me—"

"Oh, spare me! Look at you in your nice suit, working for a hotsy law firm. You never would have talked to me."

Why am I talking to you now? Why did you bring me here?

He clenched both fists. "You made out like a fucking bandit!"

"No!" I'd had a wider range of options to narrow, but I'd done it. For three years, I'd done it.

He pressed his fists to his eyes. It took me a moment to realize he was crying. Then his hands dropped. From his jacket pocket he drew a small bundle wrapped in a red kerchief. He held it to his temple.

He said, "I wanted you to see this."

I had no idea what he was doing. It was unreal and I was incorporeal.

Not even the blast tipped me off. And when David Williams fell, the bundle arcing out of his hand, I thought he'd suffered a sudden failure of adrenaline.

I stood there a long time listening to grasses rustle, tree limbs creak. I stared at the dark spot on Williams's temple, the slavering laxity of his mouth, the wide-open sheen of his eyes.

I moved toward him cautiously, crouching beside him and staring. Staring and still not believing he'd shot himself right there in front of me. When I finally did believe it, I crawled away, scrambling at first on all fours like an animal. Then I ran, ran like hell down the hill, away from him.

Before I reached the woods, a huge man caught me with a flying tackle, knocking the air out of my lungs.

I spat out a mouthful of grit, struggled against the hands on my arms, tried to see through tears and dust.

I panted, "Man shot himself. Up there."

"What I saw was you crouched over him. I think you better wait right here."

And wait I did, with the real Jerry Reiner frog-marching me back to the house so he could phone 911.

"Do I have to tell you again how it happened?"

Roland Tsieh examined the small room with interest. The Santa Cruz County Jail complex was relatively new. Winship, McAuliffe, Potter & Tsieh had never had a client there before. The tall man with the almond eyes and a supercilious face seemed pleased with me, for once; more pleased than he'd ever been when I'd worked for him.

He nodded. "From the time he's waiting for you in Reiner's driveway."

Roland listened attentively as I went through it again.

"Roland, the physical evidence supports my story, doesn't it?"

"The physical evidence. We have one small-caliber gun wrapped in a handkerchief about four feet from the body—yes, yes, I know it flew out of his hand when he fell. But basically the gun's right where you were standing. It's unregistered—and you are known to have connections with unsavory people like passport forgers, so presumably you could have obtained such a weapon. Also, which I did not realize, you know how to shoot a gun." He shrugged. "Mainly, though, it's who he was. The evil prison guard who let your pet client get killed. That's really why you're in here."

"But I didn't know who he was until I got there. He told me he was Jerry Reiner!"

"That's what you say. It could have been the other way around. You setting up a meeting with him."

"He phoned John Cusinich and pretended he was Jerry Reiner. We can prove that."

"We can prove *someone* did that. It could have been you as easily as Williams. In fact, damn clever, if you'd set it up—you can't make the shooting look like suicide, you claim self-defense. Big guy lures you to the mountains."

"But John Cusinich—"

"Credible lawyer that he is, says he fixed you up with a 'client' who claimed to be Reiner but wasn't." Roland nodded. "Makes it look like Williams set a trap for you. Except you know what the prosecution will say: it could have been any man on the phone. It could have been your passport forger."

Passport forger—again Roland raked me with the words.

"How can they get a motive out of this, Roland? Just because Williams was on duty when they killed Raul—"

"Just because? Hell, Alegria dies and you're in deep mourning for three years." He looked startled by my tears. "You never said anything to anyone about that, did you? Never complained that the guard was an SOB?"

"Only to Raul's mother."

"Great! I can just see her on the witness stand, adding her own bit of venom as she repeats what you said. Anyone else?"

I shook my head.

Roland stood. "You've got the money, I assume? Your ten percent?" I could get ninety percent of the bail money from a bailbondsman. The rest would come out of my pocket. "If the bail's under twenty thousand."

"Twenty thou!" he scoffed. "Five times that, if we're lucky."

Bail was set at $350,000. It was set unusually high because I had "so recently" demonstrated my willingness to abet a flight from prosecution.

Brad Palmer put up my ten percent. Even in his salary range, it must have hurt to write a check for thirty-five thousand dollars.

I said, "Thank you. I'd have gone nuts in jail."

He said, "I knew that three years ago."

I held his hand, cold and creamed, but it felt like lizard skin to me. I couldn't imagine ever having loved him. I felt nothing but tolerance and distance. But I was glad he'd put up my bail.

It helped square things between us. Close the accounts.

Because Brad would lose his bail money. Just as I would lose the money I'd spent getting back my license.

I couldn't stick around. I'd been a criminal lawyer too long. I'd watched guilty men go free and nice men go to prison. I'd watched a client die slowly because a cynical guard wouldn't lift a hand to help him. (Yes, I did blame Williams. More than ever.) I wouldn't risk my freedom, my life.

I still knew where to find the passport forger I'd contacted for Raul. The minute Roland Tsieh mentioned him, I knew I'd go see him.

God knew where I'd go from there. Someplace lusher than Fairfield; I would give myself a break, this time. And I was almost used to drifting along without a career.

Maybe when she heard what happened, Martina Alegria would buy another Mass for me.

Do Not Resuscitate

She awakened with a prickle of dread like sharp-nailed fingers up her side. Then she closed her eyes again, closed them tight. One of her inner voices, sweet and coaxing, usually reserved for Hank, her husband of five years, chastised: Oh honey, don't squish your face up. If Hank's watching, he's going to think you look like one of those dolls with dried apples for heads.

Not that Hank would think any such thing. But she always made sure he couldn't think anything crueler than she'd already thought herself: that way, she was dejinxed, protected. No matter that she didn't need protection.

She'd married Hank, seventy-three to her fifty-one, because he was absolutely devoted and uncritical of her, a big leathery old cowboy with a quick smile and a generous nature and, until his hard stroke three years ago, had a wonderful body for a man his age. Even with the stroke, his good conditioning and can-do attitude had brought him most of the way back. It had been a hellish few years, but except for kind of a pinched look on the left side of his face and some stiltedness in his walk, he was still her lean, mean ranching machine.

Just thinking of him soothed her unattributed anxiety on this chill November morning. She reached a plump, languid arm across the bed, feeling for Hank. Nothing. She fanned the arm as if making a snow angel. How odd: the sheets were cold. Whyever would the sheets be cold?

In fact, her whole body was cold. That was the sensation she'd translated into prickling apprehension.

She realized she was uncovered. "Hank?" She could hear panic in her voice. This was too much like three years ago, when his middle-of-the-night stroke had sent him sliding off the bed, dragging the satin comforter with him.

She'd awakened then to find him on the floor, murmuring vaguely and disjointedly about having rolled off. But she could tell by the temperature of the sheets that he'd rolled off much earlier in the night. And besides, why hadn't he gotten back up? She'd dialed 911 with trembling fingers, seeing that his right side was frozen into a fetal curve. And that he'd wet himself. And that half his face had collapsed into a slack mask.

She'd been scared to death, of course, scared of losing him. Hank was the only one in her endlessly dreary life who'd loved her right. Not that it had been perfect. Not that she hadn't cried rivers over his first wife, whom she couldn't bear to hear about even for a second. Not that she hadn't offered to let him go the time that cute neighbor was making a play for him, or the time that his ex-sister-in-law was bawling on his shoulder because her boy got shot.

Every time she saw him with a pretty woman it was torture. He was so good and so wonderful. And she wasn't much, no indeed. Not much on looks, not much on brains, disorganized, bad with money, always buying shoes that turned out not to fit or antiques that turned out to be fakes. And she didn't get Hank's jokes sometimes. And she couldn't keep track of politics even when they affected ranch business.

It was like her brother always used to say: if she was a fish, anybody would throw her back. She used to try to tag after her big brother, she loved him so. But he'd play with anybody anywhere anytime to get away from her, and he took every chance to let her know she was ugly and stupid and boring. And her parents, though they tried to give her love, couldn't help but love her brother better. They showed off his report cards and athletic trophies, and they laughed at his quick wit, and later when he became a magazine writer, they kept a leather scrapbook of his stories.

They'd been good folk. It wasn't their fault they couldn't find anything to admire in their dumbish lump of a daughter who kept living at home even into her forties without much to say for herself, bringing round one mean-tempered boyfriend after another who used her for sex with one eye out at all times for a cuter prospect.

And then, just when things seemed hopeless, she'd met Hank. A temporary secretarial agency had sent her here to this sprawling house to help him catch up on his bookkeeping and paperwork.

She'd fallen for him at first sight. He had lines of good temper leathered right into his face. He was ranch scruffy and unpretentiously willing to sit and listen to her chatter. He even laughed at her lame jokes. And he told her the first time he heard her say it that she was absolutely wrong about being fat; he thought she looked just right.

From their very first date, she'd felt guilty. Oh lord, she was wasting his evening. She'd look around the restaurant and see all the women her age who'd kept their figures and had the most refined expressions on their faces, and she'd think, He should be with her, not me. She deserves him. If he wasn't with me tonight, someone better would have him.

She brought it up a few times, but it seemed to make him mad. He didn't understand at first how hard it was for her.

For instance, at first, he used to talk about his dead wife. They'd gotten married when they were nineteen and stayed married thirty years, until she was killed in a car crash. He'd never gotten over it, he told her.

She'd burst into tears. He'd thought then that she was just

tenderhearted, but it wasn't that. It was that Missy, the first wife, should still have him. She was clearly so far superior that it wasn't even right she should be living in Missy's house or riding in the four-wheeler Missy had bought.

Every time he mentioned Missy, it tore her apart. She would cry in secret for days. She would try to harden her heart toward Hank so that the relationship would die out and he could be left with the memory of that deserving woman instead of the reality of stupid, inadequate her.

When it finally dawned on Hank what was happening, he tried to talk it over with her, insisting that it didn't lessen his feelings for her to have loved someone else once. But when he said that, it was like cold steel in her heart. She only wanted to pack her things and flee. She could see he tolerated her out of kindness, and that that must be torture to a heart that had known the love of Missy.

For a while, he was angry at her. He'd been married thirty years, he cried. Was he supposed to never mention anything that happened in all that time because it involved Missy? That was silly. That was unfair to him. She needed to get it over it.

He sounded just like her brother when he screamed at her that way. "Leave me alone, fatty! Tag after someone else for a change! Get a life!"

It hurt her even more when Hank finally accepted she'd never be able to deal with it. He stopped speaking Missy's name. Talked about his past only in ways that made no hint of Missy's presence. It was so artificial and obvious, it just about killed her. She'd wrecked part of his joy and happiness by being stupid about things. Knowing that was constant hell. And yet she couldn't get past it, couldn't hear Missy's name—or not hear it when it should have been mentioned— without turning inside out.

She'd had some bitter cries over the years, wanting desperately to find the strength to release Hank, to give him the chance to find a saner, nicer woman.

Every time they met a woman she liked, in fact, it hurt her terribly. She should let Hank go, and she knew it. She didn't deserve him.

And yet, selfishly, she was grateful he ignored her altruistic outbursts. But she watched him grow more and more wary of them, more and more careful of what he said and how he acted in company, because the least show of social warmth made her sure she should step out of his life right now. And feeling that way, she'd get all fragile and crazy, secretly searching his pockets and papers, or crawling to her corner of the bed and not letting Hank near her.

After Hank's first stroke, when she had to nurse him and help him, and it seemed like another woman might not want to, then they'd finally found some happiness. For a long time, his speech had been slurred, so he hadn't been able to blunder into emotionally mined territory. She'd helped him in every way she could then, feeling a ferocious sympathy for his torment. He'd always been so active, poor darling, riding the ranch, splitting the wood, mending the fences. It had been torture for him, a year in a wheelchair, another year with a walker. He'd only put his cane aside last month.

And now here she was, lying uncovered on the bed again. And she was scared, too scared to move. Because he'd begged her: if it ever happened again, she mustn't let them save him. At his age, he'd never be able to come back to anywhere near the point he was now, not again. And he couldn't survive the immobility, not again. For him, it was the worst claustrophobia.

He'd had a lawyer write him up a piece of paper saying if he ever got to the point where he was too sick to live productively, he wanted to die naturally. He didn't want machines and chemicals keeping his body alive if he couldn't use it.

In the abstract, she understood. She felt that way about herself, too. Especially after seeing all poor Hank had suffered, with a tube up his nose for food and liquids, and a catheter in him, and bruises on his body, and sores under his eyes because they teared uncontrollably.

But on the other hand, with her to help him, he'd made it back the first time. And for once, she'd felt really useful and special. Almost worthy of his love and company.

All this went through her mind in a flash when she made her snow angel arm sweep and felt the bed cold and empty. But maybe it was just a knee jerk of dread to ward off the jinx. She always did think the worst thing first, to get it over. Maybe Hank was okay, maybe in the kitchen having early oolong.

But this time it didn't feel like she was just being silly. Nearly frozen with cold and fear, she scooted her size forty-two pink pajamas across the bed, peering over the edge as if over the cliffs of hell.

Her heart felt like a hot rock in her chest: There he was on the floor.

"Hank! Oh, Hank . . ." Her voice bled.

She slid down beside him.

He looked so old, her wonderful Hank. His eyes were half-shut and his mouth was open with his tongue tip protruding. His skin looked yellow, settling into deep caverns beneath his stubbled cheekbones. His breaths were the shallowest rasps, his lips were turning blue. She'd never seen him look so dreadful, not even that other awful morning.

With a thin wail, she reached a multiply-ringed hand toward the antique-reproduction phone by the bedside, the one that replaced Missy's pink princess, just as she'd replaced all Missy's furniture and fittings. She dialed 911, and cried for a while into the mouthpiece before she could even speak.

When she knew the paramedics were coming, she sank back beside Hank and stroked his cold face. He was barely breathing. He looked almost dead. His pupils, visible through half-open eyes, were different sizes.

Months ago, the doctors had warned her. The blood thinners he took every day since his stroke would keep Hank from having another stroke from a blood clot, but if he had the kind caused by bleeding in the brain, the anticoagulants would make the stroke worse. The bleeding in his head would go on and on, killing more and more brain cells, leaving only random sparks of consciousness in a paralyzed body.

To Hank it was the ultimate horror story. Don't ever forget, he told her a thousand times. If the paramedics come, show them the paper in the nightstand drawer. Don't let them do anything to save me. I couldn't take it, honey, it'd be living hell. Even weak from his first stroke, he'd grabbed her shoulders tight and shaken them. Don't let them keep me alive in hell, honey. Don't let them.

She watched him now, frozen in a twilight of impending loneliness. She reached a hand to the drawer and withdrew the paper. DO NOT RESUSCITATE, it read across the top. She slipped it into her pajama pocket, lost in swirling memories of his kindness and maleness and devotedness.

"Oh Hank," she whispered. "I always loved you so so much, I always wanted you to be happy and have everything you deserved. I'll never be happy without you, Hank."

There was a sudden flutter in his breathing. "Pain," he gurgled, his voice a wet, small croak of a thing, "Gone. Can't feel body."

She knew in her heart what he was telling her, what he was begging her. Begging her to remember the paper in the drawer.

"I'll do what you asked, Hank. How could I not?"

"Missy," he choked. "Aw, look what a gorgeous girl I married."

She drew back as if slapped. What she'd always feared: Missy was the one, the gorgeous one love of Hank's life. Missy's name on his lips now! After she'd finally convinced herself he loved *her!* That her nursing had made her worthy of him.

"Coming, Missy." His voice was louder now. His eyelids fluttered open, and he stared ahead with mismatched pupils. "Coming back to you now, my beauty."

She looked down at him, frozen in her vortex of rejection. It always came back to this: every man had left her for someone. As soon as there was someone else to be with, he was gone—every man starting with her own brother.

And now Hank, too.

"Remember. . . ." His speech was slurring, fading. "Dancing in Paris?"

She'd refused to go to Europe on a honeymoon because he'd been there with Missy. Everything everywhere would remind him of Missy, she was sure. So they'd gone to Florida, which he hadn't much liked because she was always too hot and tired to do anything.

" 'Member? Alps? Walking?"

He looked at her and his face, so cold white and skeletally sunken, managed to wear the faint ghost of an old happiness.

"Coming back to you, Missy . . ." Then he stopped breathing. Just stopped. Grew more pale and almost blue.

For what seemed an eternity, she watched him. She imagined his soul rising to embrace the beautiful, fun-loving, intelligent mate of his spirit, the incomparable Missy. She saw them laughing and happy and full of tears and remembrances, with not a backward glance for her.

God, how it tore at her! How wrong she'd been to tell herself she should let him go to someone who deserved him. It wasn't true. It had never been true. She didn't care who deserved him. She wanted him, fiercely and with her whole heart. And she didn't care if she didn't deserve him. He was hers. She had loved him and nursed him. She had finally earned him.

She screamed when she heard the doorbell. Then, walking as if with a twisting knife in her back, she stumbled to the doorway.

In their police-like uniforms, two paramedics stood before her. She waved her arm behind her, hot tears spilling down her cheeks.

She remained rooted in the doorway while they pushed past her with their bags and plastic devices.

She trailed behind them finally and overheard one of them mutter, "Not good!"

While his partner inserted a plastic tube into Hank's mouth, he looked over his shoulder. "We're going to try to resuscitate him. How long has he been this way?"

"Stopped breathing, oh God." Her voice was a foolish twitter. "Minutes ago. Maybe five?"

The paramedic shook his head again. "There'll be substantial deficits if he does recover. Permanent brain injuries. He could be a vegetable." It was said kindly, for all the harshness of the message. "Do you know if he has a Do Not Resuscitate order on file at the hospital?"

She stopped breathing herself for that moment. She saw him dancing in Paris with Missy. It was wrong, it was too late; he was her husband now, not Missy's. "I don't think so," she whispered.

"He doesn't have a document around here saying he doesn't want to be resuscitated in a situation like this?" The

Lia Matera

paramedic seemed to be appealing to her. Telling her Hank's fate would be a cruel one if he lived.

Her hand went to the document in her pocket. "I can't give him up." And yet she always thought she could and should give him up, give him to someone worthy of him, someone like Missy. It was he who had always insisted they remain together in spite of her "jealousies." Now it was clear: she'd hung on as hard as she could every step of the way. And she'd hang on now. "He'd want you to save his life," she said. "He'd want you to try, no matter what."

And she watched the paramedic attach a bellowslike bag to the tube in Hank's throat. She watched Hank's chest rise and fall, rise and fall until a bit of color returned to his cheeks.

There would be no dancing with Missy today. Missy was not his wife anymore. She was.

The River Mouth

To reach the mouth of the Klamath River, you head west off 101 just south of the Oregon border. You hike through an old Yurok meeting ground, an overgrown glade with signs asking you to respect native spirits and stay out of the cooking pits and the split-log amphitheater. The trail ends at a sand cliff. From there you can watch the Klamath rage into the sea, battering the tide. Waves break in every direction, foam blowing off like rising ghosts. Sea lions by the dozens bob in the swells, feeding on eels flushed out of the river.

My boyfriend and I made our way down to the wet clay beach. The sky was every shade of gray, and the Pacific looked like mercury. We were alone except for five Yurok in rubber boots and checkered flannel, fishing in the surf. We watched them flick stiff whips of sharpened wire mounted on pick handles. When the tips lashed out of the waves, they had eels impaled on them. With a rodeo windup, they flipped the speared fish over their shoulders into pockets they'd dug in the sand. We passed shallow pits seething with creatures that looked like short, mean-faced snakes.

We continued for maybe a quarter mile beyond the river mouth. We climbed some small, sharp rocks to get to a tall, flat one midway between the shore and the cliff. From there we could see the fishermen but not have our conversation carry down to them.

Our topic of the day (we go to the beach to hash things out) was if we wanted to get married. Because it was a big, in-

79

timidating topic, we'd driven almost four hundred miles to find the right beach. We'd had to spend the night in a tacky motel, but this was the perfect spot, no question.

Patrick uncorked the champagne—we had two bottles; it was likely to be a long talk. I set out the canned salmon and crackers on paper plates on the old blue blanket. I kicked off my shoes so I could cross my legs. I watched Pat pour, wondering where we'd end up on the marriage thing.

When he handed me the paper cup of bubbles, I tapped it against his. "To marriage or not."

"To I do or I don't," he agreed.

The air smelled like cold beach, like wet sky and slick rocks and storms coming. At home, the beach stinks like fish and shored seaweed buzzing with little flies. If there are sunbathers on blankets, you can smell their beer and coconut oil.

"So, Pat?" I looked him over, trying to imagine being married to him. He was a freckly, baby-faced Scot with strange hair and hardly any meat on him. Whereas I was a black-haired mutt who tended to blimp out in the winter and get it back under control in the summer. But the diets were getting harder, and I knew fat women couldn't be choosers. I was thinking it was time to lock in. And worrying that was an unworthy motive. "Maybe we're fine the way we are now."

Right away he frowned.

"I just mean it's okay with me the way it is."

"Because you were married to Mr. Perfect and how could I ever take his place?"

"Hearty-har." Mr. Perfect meaning my ex-husband had plenty of money and good clothes. Pat had neither right now. He'd just got laid off, and there were a thousand other software engineers answering every ad he did.

"I guess *he* wasn't an 'in-your-face child,' " Pat added.

Aha. Here we had last night's fight.

"With Mr. Perfect you didn't even have arguments. He knew when to stop."

Me and Pat fight on long drives. I say things. I don't necessarily mean them. It was too soon to call the caterer, I guess.

I held out my paper cup for more. "All I meant was he had more experience dealing with—"

"Oh, it goes without saying!" He poured refills so fast they bubbled over. "I'm a mere infant! About as cleanly as a teenager and as advanced in my political analysis as a college freshman."

"What is this, a retrospective of old fights? Okay, so it takes some adjustment living with a person. I've said things in crabby moments. On the drive up—"

"Crabby moments? You? No, you're an *artist*." You could have wrung the scorn out of the word and still had it drip sarcasm. "Reality's just more *complicated* for you."

I felt my eyes narrow. "I hate that, Patrick."

"Oh, she's calling me Patrick."

Usually I got formal when I got mad. "I'm not in the best mood when I write. If you could just learn to leave me alone then." Like I said in the car.

His pale brows pinched as he flaked salmon onto crackers. I made a show of shading my eyes and watching a Yurok woman walk toward us. When she got to the bottom of our rock, she called up, "Got a glass for me?"

Usually we were antisocial, which is why we did our drinking at the beach instead of in bars. But the conversation wasn't going the greatest. A diversion, a few minutes to chill—why not?

"Sure," I said.

Pat hit me with the angry-bull look, face lowered, brows down, nostrils flared. As she clattered up the rocks, he muttered, "I thought we came here to be alone."

"Hi there," she said, reaching the top. She was slim, maybe forty, with long brown hair and a semi-flat nose and darkish skin just light enough to show some freckles. She had a great smile but bad teeth. She wore a black hat almost like a cowboy's but not as western. She sat on a wet part of the rock to spare our blanket whatever funk was on her jeans (as if we cared).

"Picnic, huh? Great spot."

I answered, "Yeah," because Pat was sitting in pissy silence.

She drank some champagne. "Not many people know about this beach. You expecting other folks?"

"No. We're pretty far from home."

"This is off the beaten path, all right." She glanced over her shoulder, waving at her friends.

"We had to hike through Yurok land to get here," I admitted. "Almost elven, and that wonderful little amphitheater." I felt embarrassed, didn't know how to assure her we hadn't been disrespectful. I'd had to relieve myself behind a bush, but we didn't do war cries or anything insensitive. "I hope it isn't private property. I hope this beach isn't private."

"Nah. That'd be a crime against nature, wouldn't it?" She grinned. "There's a trailer park up the other way. That *is* private property. But as long as you go out the way you came in, no problem."

"Thanks, that's good to know. We heard about this beach on our last trip north, but we didn't have a chance to check it out. We didn't expect all the seals or anything."

"Best time of year; eels come upriver to spawn in the ocean. Swim twenty-five hundred miles, some of them," she explained. "It's a holy spot for the Yurok, the river mouth." A break in the clouds angled light under her hat brim, showing leathery lines around her eyes. "This place is about mouths, really. In the river, the eel is the king mouth. He hides, he waits, he strikes fast. But time comes when he's got to heed that urge. And he swims right into the jaws of the sea lion. Yup." She motioned behind her. "Here and now, this is the eel's judgment day."

Pat was giving me crabby little get-rid-of-her looks. I ignored him. Okay, we had a lot to talk about. But what are the odds of a real-McCoy Yurok explaining the significance of a beach?

She lay on her side on the blanket, holding out her paper cup for a refill and popping some salmon into her mouth. "Salmon means renewal," she said. "Carrying on the life cycle, all that. You should try the salmon jerky from the rancheria."

Pat hesitated before refilling her cup. I let him fill mine too.

"King mouth of the river, that's the eel," she repeated. "Of course, the Eel River's named after him. But it's the Klamath that's his castle. They'll stay alive out of water longer than any other fish I know. You see them flash that ugly gray-green in the surf, and thwack, you get them on your whipstick and flip them onto the pile. You do that awhile, you know, and get maybe fifteen, and when you go back to put them in your bucket, maybe eight of the little monsters have managed to jump out of the pit and crawl along the sand. You see how far some of them got and you have to think they stayed alive a good half hour out of the water. Now how's that possible?"

I lay on my side too, sipping champagne, listening, watching the gorgeous spectacle behind her in the distance: seals bobbing and diving, the river crashing into the sea, waves colliding like hands clapping. Her Yurok buddies weren't fishing anymore, they were talking. One gestured toward our rock. I kind of hoped they'd join us. Except Pat would really get cranky then.

Maybe I did go too far on the drive up. But I wished he'd let it go.

"So it's not much of a surprise, huh?" the woman continued. "That they're king of the river. They're mean and tough, they got teeth like nails. If they were bigger, man, sharks wouldn't stand a chance, never mind seals." She squinted at me, sipping. "Because the cussed things can hide right in the open. Their silt-barf color, they can sit right in front of a rock, forget behind it. They can look like part of the scenery. And you swim by feeling safe and cautious, whoever you are—maybe some fancy fish swum upriver—and munch! You're eel food. But the river ends somewhere, you know what I mean? Every river has its mouth. There's always that bigger mouth out there waiting for you to wash in, no matter how sly and bad you are at home. You heed those urges and leave your territory, and you're dinner."

Pat was tapping the bottom of my foot with his. Tapping, tapping urgently like I should do something.

That's when I made up my mind: Forget marriage. He was too young. Didn't want to hear this Yurok woman talk and was tapping on me like, Make her go away, Mom. I had kids, two of them, and they were grown now and out of the house. And not much later, their dad went too (though I didn't miss him and I did miss the kids, at least sometimes). And I didn't need someone fifteen years younger than me always putting the responsibility on me. I paid most of the bills, got the food together (didn't cook, but knew my delis), picked up around the house, told Pat what he should read because engineers don't know squat about literature or history; and every time someone needed getting rid of or something social had to be handled or even just a business letter had to be written, it was tap-tap-tap, oh, Maggie, could you please . . . ?

I reached behind me and shoved Pat's foot away. If he wanted to be antisocial, he could think of a way to make the woman leave himself. We had plenty of time to talk, just the two of us. I didn't want her to go yet.

"Got any more?" the Yurok asked.

I pulled the second bottle out of our beat-up backpack and opened it, trying not to look at Pat, knowing he'd have that hermity scowl now big-time.

"You picnic like this pretty often?" she asked.

"Yeah, we always keep stuff in the trunk—wine, canned salmon, crackers. Gives us the option." That was the other side of it: Pat was fun, and he let me have control. If I said let's go, he said okay. That means everything if you spent twenty years with a stick-in-the-mud.

"You come here a lot?" she asked.

"No. This was a special trip."

"It was supposed to be," Pat fussed.

I hastily added, "Our beaches down around Santa Cruz and Monterey are nice, but we've been to them a thousand times."

"Mmm." She let me refill her cup. I had more too. Pat didn't seem to be drinking.

"Now, the sea lion is a strange one," she said. "There's little it won't eat, and not much it won't do to survive, but it has no guile. It swims along, do-de-do, and has a bite whenever it can. It doesn't hide or trick. It's lazy. If it can find a place to gorge, it'll do that and forget about hunting. It doesn't seem to have the hunting instinct. It just wants to eat and swim and jolly around. Mate. Be playful." She broke another piece of salmon off, holding it in fingers with silt and sand under the nails. "Whereas an eel is always lurking, even when it's just eaten. It never just cavorts. It's always thinking ahead, like a miser worrying how to get more."

"Until it leaves home and washes into the sea lion's mouth." I concluded the thought for her.

"What the eel needs"—she sat up—"is a way to say, Hell no. Here it is, the smarter, stealthier creature. And what does nature do but use its own instinct against it. Favor some fat, lazy thing that's not even a fish, it's a mammal that lives in the water, that doesn't really belong and yet has food poured down its gullet just for being in the right place." She pointed at the sea lion heads bobbing in the waves. "Look at them. This is their welfare cafeteria. They do nothing but open their mouths."

Pat put in, "You could say you're like the seals. You're out there with those steel-pronged things, spearing eels."

I wanted to hit him. It seemed a rude thing to say.

"The Yurok are like the eels." She removed her hat. Her dark hair, flattened on top, began to blow in the wind coming off the water. "The Yurok were king because the Yurok knew how to blend in. The Yurok thought always of food for to-morrow because Yurok nightmares were full of yesterday's starvation. The Yurok were part of the dark bottom of history's river, silent and ready. And they got swept out into the bigger mouths that waited without deserving."

She leaped to her feet. She looked majestic, her hair blowing against a background of gray-white clouds, her arms and chin raised to the heavens. "This is where the ancient river meets the thing that is so much bigger, the thing the eel can't bear to understand because the knowledge is too bitter."

Behind me, Pat whispered, "This is weird. Look at her friends."

On the beach, the Yurok men raised their arms too. They stood just like the woman, maybe imitating her to tease her, maybe just coincidence.

"Where the ancient river meets the thing that is much bigger, and the eel can't understand because the knowledge is too bitter," she repeated to the sky.

Pat was poking me now, hardly bothering to whisper. "I don't like this! She's acting crazy!"

I smacked him with an absentminded hand behind my back, like a horse swatting off a fly. Maybe this was too much for a software engineer—why had I ever thought I could marry someone as unlyrical as that?—but it was a writer's dream. It was real-deal Yurok lore. If she quit because of him, I'd push Pat's unimaginative damn butt right off the rock.

She shook her head from side to side, hair whipping her cheeks. "At the mouth of the river, you learn the truth: Follow your obsession, and the current carries you into a hundred waiting mouths. But if you lie quiet"—she bent forward so I could see her bright dark eyes—"and think passionately of trapping your prey, if your hunger is a great gnawing within you, immobilizing you until the moment when you become a rocket of appetite to consume what swims near—"

"What do they want?" Pat's shadow fell across the rock. I turned to see that he was standing now, staring down the beach at the Yurok men.

They'd taken several paces toward us. They seemed to be watching the woman.

She was on a roll, didn't even notice. "Then you don't ride the river into the idle mouth, the appetite without intelligence, the hunger that happens without knowing itself."

Pat's anoraked arm reached over me and plucked the paper cup from her hand. "You better leave now."

"What is your problem, Patrick?" I jumped to my feet. Big damn kid, Jesus Christ. Scared by legends, by champagne talk on a beach! "Mellow the hell out."

My words wiped the martial look off his face. A marveling betrayal replaced it. "You think you're so smart, Maggie, you think you know everything! But you're really just a sheltered little housewife."

I was too angry to speak. I maybe hadn't earned much over the years, but I was a *writer*.

His lips compressed, his eyes squinted, his whole freckled Scot's face crimped with wronged frustration. "But I guess the Mature One has seen more than a child like myself. I guess it takes an Artist to really know life."

"Oh, for Christ sake!" I spoke the words with both arms and my torso. "Are you such a white-bread baby you can't hear a little bit of Yurok metaphor without freaking out?"

He turned, began to clamber down the rock. He was muttering. I caught the words "princess" and "know everything," as well as some serious profanity.

I turned to find the Yurok woman sitting on the blanket, drinking sedately, her posture unabashedly terrible. I remained standing for a few minutes, watching Patrick jerk along the beach, fists buried in his pockets.

"He doesn't want my friends to join us," she concluded correctly. From the look of it, he was marching straight over to tell them so.

The men stood waiting. A hundred yards behind them, desperate eels wriggled from their sand pits like the rays of a sun.

I had a vision of roasting eels with the Yuroks, learning their legends as the waves crashed beside us. What a child Pat was. Just because we'd fought a bit in the car.

"I know why he thinks I'm crazy," the woman said.

I sat with a sigh, pulling another paper cup out of the old backpack and filling it. I handed it to her, feeling like shit. So what if the men wanted to join us for a while? Patrick and I had the rest of the afternoon to fight. Maybe the rest of our lives.

"We came out here to decide if we should get married," I told her. I could feel tears sting my eyes. "But the trouble is, he's still so young. He's only seven years older than my oldest daughter. He doesn't have his career together—he just got laid off. He's been moping around all month getting in my way. He's an engineer—I met him when I was researching a science fiction story. All he knows about politics and litera- ture is what I've made him learn." I wiped the tears. "He's grown a lot in the last year, since we've been together, but it's not like being with an equal. I mean, we have a great time unless we start talking about something in particular, and then I have to put up with all these half-baked, college- student kind of ideas. I have to give him articles to read and tell him how to look at things—I mean, yes, he's smart, obviously, and a quick learner. But fifteen years, you know."

She nibbled a bit more salmon. "Probably he saw the van on the road coming down."

"What van?"

"Our group."

"The Yurok?"

She wrinkled her nose. "No. They're up in Hoopa on the reservation, what's left of them. They're practically extinct."

"We assumed you were Yurok. You're all so dark. You know how to do that whip-spear thing."

"Yeah, we're all dark-haired." She rolled her eyes. "But jeez, there's only five of us. You're dark-haired. You're not Yurok." Her expression brightened. "But the whipstick, that's Yurok, you're right. Our leader"—she pointed to the not-Yuroks on the beach, I wasn't sure which one—"made them. We're having an out-of-culture experience, you could say."

Patrick had reached the group now, was standing with his shoulders up around his ears and his hands still buried in his pockets.

"How did you all get so good at it?"

"Good at it?" She laughed. "The surf's absolutely crawling with eels. If we were good at it, we'd have hundreds of them."

"What's the group?"

Patrick's hands were out of his pockets now. He held them out in front of him as he began backing away from the four men.

"You didn't see the van, really?"

"Maybe Pat did. I was reading the map." I rose to my knees, watching him. Patrick was still backing away, picking up speed. Up here, showing fear of a ranting woman, he'd seemed ridiculous. Down on the beach, with four long-haired men advancing toward him, his fear arguably had some basis. What had they said to him?

"The van scares people." She nodded. "The slogans we painted on it."

"Who are you?" I asked her, eyes still locked on Patrick.

"I was going to say before your fiancé huffed out: What about the sea lions? They get fat with no effort, just feasting on the self-enslaved, black-souled little eels. Do they get away with it?"

The sky was beginning to darken. The sea was pencil-lead gray now, with a bright silver band along the horizon. Patrick was running toward us across the beach.

Two of the men started after him.

I tried to rise to my feet, but the woman clamped her hand around my ankle.

"No," she said. "The sea lions aren't happy very long. They're just one more fat morsel in the food chain. Offshore there are sharks, plenty of them, the mightiest food processors of all. This is their favorite spot for sea lion sushi."

"What are they doing? What do your friends want?" My voice was as shrill as the wind whistling between the rocks.

"The Yurok were the eels, kings of the river, stealthy and quick and hungry. But the obsessions of history washed them into the jaws of white men, who played and gorged in the surf." She nodded. "The ancient river meets the thing that is much bigger, the thing the eel can't bear to understand because the knowledge is too bitter."

She'd said that more than once, almost the same way. Maybe that's what scared Pat: her words were like a litany, an incantation, some kind of cultish chant. And the men below had mirrored her gestures.

I knocked her hand off my ankle and started backward off the rock. All she'd done was talk about predation. She'd learned we were alone and not expecting company, and she'd signaled to the men on the beach. Now they were chasing Patrick.

Afraid to realize what it meant, too rattled to put my shoes back on, I stepped into a slick crevice. I slid, losing my balance. I fell, racketing over the brutal jags and edges of the smaller rocks we'd used as a stairway. I could hear Patrick scream my name. I felt a lightning burn of pain in my ribs, hip, knee. I could feel the hot spread of blood under my shirt.

I tried to catch my breath, to stand up. The woman was picking her way carefully down to where I lay.

"There's another kind of hunter, Maggie." I could hear the grin in her voice. "Not the eel who waits and strikes. Not the seal who finds plenty and feeds. But the shark." She stopped, silhouette poised on the rock stair. "Who thinks of nothing but finding food, who doesn't just hide like the eel or wait like the sea lion but who quests and searches voraciously, looking for another—"

Patrick screamed, but not my name this time.

"Looking for a straggler." Again she raised her arms and her chin to the heavens, letting her dark hair fly around her. Patrick was right, she did look crazy.

She jumped down. Patrick screamed again. We screamed together, finally in agreement.

I heard a sudden blast and knew it must be gunfire. I watched the woman land in a straddling crouch, her hair in wild tendrils like eels wriggling from their pits.

Oh, Patrick. Let me turn back the clock and say I'm sorry.

I looked up at the woman, thinking: Too late, too late. I rode the river right into your jaws.

Another shot. Did it hit Pat?

A voice from the sand cliff boomed, "Get away!"

The woman looked up and laughed. She raised her arms again, throwing back her head.

A third blast sent her scrambling off the small rocks, kicking up footprints in the sand as she ran away. She waved her arms as if to say goodbye.

I sat painfully forward—I'd cracked a rib, broken some skin. I could feel it. Nevertheless, I twisted to look up the face of the cliff.

In the blowing grass above me, a stocky man with long black hair fired a rifle into the air.

A real Yurok, Pat and I learned later.

Performance Crime

I was about as stressed out as I could be. In addition to my work year starting at the university, I was trying to help get the Moonjuice Performance Gallery's new show together. After last year's fiasco, Moonjuice needed something accessible. And that would never happen unless someone displayed some sense, however tame that might seem to the artists.

But the artists weren't the main problem, the main problem was Moonjuice's board of directors. The "conservative" members were two wannabe-radical university professors. The middle-of-the-roaders were a desktop publisher and an aspiring blues guitarist. On the avant-garde extreme was self-proclaimed bad girl and dabbling artist Georgia Stepp. I, an untenured associate professor, was so far to the right of other board members it was laughable. I was a fiscally responsible Democrat, which practically opened me to charges of fascism.

I was trying to make my point about being sensible to Georgia.

"We have to be careful after last year," I insisted.

"Last year was *fun*." Georgia opened her long arms for emphasis. She wore a satin camisole, emphasizing a fashionable bit of muscle. Her nails were long and black. Her blond hair was cut short and dyed black this year. "We freaked out all the prisses."

She meant "prissy" board members who'd resigned in protest, convincing our sponsors to defund us and our program advertisers to boycott us.

These were liberal restaurateurs and bookshop owners, hardly Republicans.

"We have less than a quarter of last year's budget because of that show! We've got artists working for free"—that got her—"and feminist university students volunteering elsewhere."

"Art can't follow money like a dog in heat!"

"It can't treat sponsors like fire hydrants, either. There just aren't that many patrons of the arts around," I pointed out. "Especially art by lesbians. And we lost their support over what? Way-out, nonpolitical—"

"Way-out *is* political." Georgia looked happy. And there's no one more beautiful than Georgia when she's happy. But that doesn't make her any less wrongheaded.

"Clothespins with glued-on feathers don't make a statement, I'm sorry." The "art" that made our advertisers bail included a woman in studded leather pinning feathers on her naked partner.

"It wasn't supposed to be a statement." Georgia leaned closer. "It was a dance. A dance, serious one."

"Clothespins on my nipples always make me want to dance."

"But it was about artists, not you." Georgia certainly hit the nail on the head.

"Yeah, well it wasn't about our advertisers, either. Not to mention Viv and Claire." The two former board members. "We've got to get our sponsors and advertising back, Georgia. It doesn't matter what kind of show we put on this year if no one's willing to pay for the next one. We're not Andy Hardy. We're not putting on shows to pass the summer."

She shot me a look. To her, practicality is somehow demeaning.

Marlys, legal secretary and blues guitarist, strolled in. Georgia considers her a best friend and ally. Which Marlys proved by changing the subject.

"You guys see the paper this morning?" She was short and heavy, with the usual layered haircut. The look she gave Georgia made me wonder if she minded Georgia's going to bed with every dominatrix and poet to cross our stage.

"What, daaaaarling?" Georgia liked to do Kate Hepburn, imitating gays in drag. I was never sure if I thought it was funny or disrespectful.

"Somebody broke into Greg Purl's house and shot all his cereal." Marlys was flushed, eyes sparkling as she watched Georgia.

"A cereal killer!" She practically shrieked. "Was that the point? I love it! A pun crime!"

"Plus, Greg," Marlys pointed out.

Purl was a local boy who'd made good. He'd gone to Hollywood to make big-budget lowest-common-denominator movies. His latest was about—you guessed it—the serial killer of teenage girls.

"Did the papers get it?" Georgia wondered. "Cereal killer, serial killer; his movie?"

"They got the pun." Marlys looked gratified. "They didn't really go into his movies."

Marlys and Georgia were friends with Purl before he "sold out." It always amazed me how superior they could feel, despite their obscurity and their day jobs. It's not that easy to sell out, after all. Someone has to want to buy what you've got to pander.

"Purl wasn't hurt?" Once again, mine was the lone voice of practicality.

"No, it happened at his house here. He's down in Hollywood. Someone broke in and shot his cereal boxes," Marlys explained. "According to the papers."

"How funny!" Georgia struck a pose. Give her a cigarette in a long ivory holder and she surely could be some thirties star. Or RuPaul. "Cereal killer. I'm just surprised the papers got it."

"We would have, even if they didn't." Marlys smiled.

"Was his house damaged? Did they just fire into a cupboard or what?" I loathed his last movie's relentless reliance on "sexy" violence. But that didn't give anyone the right to shoot up his kitchen. "He must feel so . . . violated."

Georgia laughed till tears sprang to her eyes. "It's almost like a Hollywood version of karma, isn't it?"

Marlys answered my question. "I guess the person took all his cereal outside and dumped it on his lawn before shooting it full of holes." She was watching Georgia, still grinning. "I knew you'd like it!"

"Well, I don't think it's funny," I put in.

Georgia cackled. "Ha! 'That's not funny'—the PC lesbian mantra."

"You're just too young to remember what it was like when everyone was politically *in*correct! It was irritating and demeaning—"

"Like political correctness," Georgia countered.

Moonjuice was going to drive me insane some day. Especially if performance artists kept embracing things we used to fight against, like pornography and the word "dyke."

"Fine, Georgia—don't get it. There's certainly plenty I don't get—like the idea of a naked choir." One of the proposed acts for our yearly fund-raiser was a naked twenty-person choir. Georgia and I had been bickering about it all afternoon. "They don't even say what they're going to sing. Like we're prurient twelve-year-olds who'll like them just because they're naked."

"Well, why not?" Georgia asked. "Haven't you ever wondered what choirgirls' breasts look like when they sing loud?"

"No!" I responded. "And I'm sure our sponsors haven't either."

"Nan's partly right," Marlys said generously. "We should judge art by itself. If they can sing, let them sing naked. If they can't, let them go streak through college campuses."

Georgia shot her an *et tu* look. "All right, all right, we'll ask them for details. But not in a philistine way."

Georgia called me at the university the next day. "Nan, come down." Down into town, where Moonjuice Gallery is.

It's a long ride to the dark little storefront full of folding chairs facing a creaky stage.

"I have students coming in forty minutes."

"Then come right away." Georgia hung up.

Georgia wouldn't be able to get away with acting like that if she looked like me. Or maybe if I had Georgia's personality, I'd look more like her, I'd be skinny and daring with strange hair and long nails.

But I didn't need Georgia's big clothing and makeup bills. I had car payments to keep up.

When I got to Moonjuice, I was surprised to see cats fighting in the empty lot across the street. It seemed ominous, somehow. But I teach classics, things tend to look symbolic to me.

When I walked into Moonjuice, I found Georgia onstage tearing through all the costumes. Feather boas were curled around her feet and spangled dresses were tossed over chairs. Some of the comedy costumes—fast food clerk, a secretary, a hockey player, a number 32 football jersey, a fireman—were strewn across the floor.

"What are you doing?" I couldn't keep exasperation out of

my voice. Who knew when we'd be able to afford new costumes? She was trashing our assets.

"I can't find anything!" She wore a black turtleneck, a tight black mini, and black stockings today. With her black nails, lips, and hair, she looked like a Parisian model for the vampire collection. "Where are the costumes from last year?"

"What costumes? You mean the whips? The clothespins?"

"The overalls, the ginghams. They've been stolen!"

She couldn't say this over the phone?

"Of course they weren't stolen," I reassured her. "Who'd want to steal gingham dresses?" Overalls maybe. "They're probably at someone's house or in the attic where they're supposed to be."

"Will you go up there and look?"

"Now?"

She nodded. "These were already down here, backstage. I can't go up to the attic—it's so dusty. My allergies."

"I'm supposed to be meeting students!"

"They'll wait."

Georgia worked nights as a cocktail waitress—but not that steadily. She always contrived to have a guest room to crash in if she couldn't make rent. To her, jobs were trifles.

She clattered down the stage steps. "Nan, please?" She linked her arm through mine. I loved the way her body felt. I know I'm not supposed to, but I get turned on by skinniness. And there just isn't that much of it in our community.

"Why do you need them?" If I relented and did this for her, I'd beat myself up over it all week. It wasn't right to put myself out for someone gorgeous if I knew I wouldn't do the same for a frumpy friend.

"I was thinking the naked choir could start out wearing them and then strip them off."

"Why?"

"I found out what they sing. They sing gospel." To her that made sense.

Don't ask me how she talked me into it. I'd be embarrassed to analyze it.

I dragged out attic boxes and searched through them. I never did find the overalls and ginghams. But I found the boxes the costumes on stage had come out of. Their paper wrappings were still scattered all around.

By the time I got back downstairs, I was late for my appointment. I tore out of there with hardly a word for Georgia. Just as well. It wouldn't have been a kind word.

On the way out, I noticed cats were still fighting across the street. The funny thing was, they were different cats this time.

When I got home from work, I showered first thing, still feeling grimy from my visit to the Moonjuice attic.

Then I ate dinner in front of the TV. I always feel guilty when I see "Kill Your Television" bumper stickers in Moonjuice's parking lot. But I work long days, deconstructing and analogizing, and dealing with students' problems. Channel surfing is my big vice.

Local news was on. "The pun-loving bandit has seemingly struck again!" The female anchor was a fluffy bit of a thing. She was my secret lust object.

I shoveled pasta into my face while she explained: "A ransom note was sent to Ygdrasil Herbs today! To ransom its *president,* you ask? No, to ransom its . . . *catnip.* That's right, *catnip*—that fragrantly psychedelic herb . . .psychedelic to *cats,* that is. Last night, someone broke into the Ygdrasil plant on Teenmore Avenue and stole their *entire stock* of catnip. Ygdrasil supplies over seventy percent of the catnip sold in this country, according to its spokesman. So better keep on kitty's *good side* for a while!"

The Ygdrasil spokesman came on the screen, explaining that the ransom note was signed "Catnip Kidnap."

The newscasters could hardly keep a straight face. "Catnip Kidnap," the airhead newswoman giggled in closing.

I thought about the cats fighting across the street from Moonjuice. It was a cat synchronicity, I guessed.

But the next day, I wasn't so sure it was a coincidence.

The media had fallen in love with their Pun-loving Bandit, reporting every conceivable connection between the Cereal Killer and the Catnip Kidnap. But that was nothing. By evening, news people were delirious with soft-news joy. Someone had stolen every meat patty from the town's most popular fast-food joint.

The first words out of the newscaster's mouth were "Burger Burglar!"

I could hardly contain my agitation as the newscaster described the burglary. The meat had been stolen during the busiest part of the lunch rush. No one had noticed anything odd. But when they went to the freezer to replenish, the patties were gone. One manager thought he'd spotted a new employee, but turnover was such that he hadn't been sure, and he'd been too busy to check.

The fast-food place had once donated a costume to Moonjuice. I'd seen it just yesterday strewn with the rest of Georgia's mess.

Georgia. She was all panache, all show. If something had style, that was enough for her. It didn't have to make sense or be wise or look good to people who mattered.

I was sure Georgia was doing it. Performance art just wasn't enough anymore. Now she'd taken to performance crime, damn her.

I wanted to strangle her. Didn't she realize these childish tricks were felonies? That she could go to prison? That

Moonjuice would sink under the scandal?

I wouldn't let it happen. I drove immediately to a mall pet store. They had very little catnip, most of it from Ygdrasil. I left it there, instead buying a small box of the other brand.

I had to go all the way across town to find another pet store open. It too had mostly Ygdrasil catnip. I bought the other brand.

Then I drove to Moonjuice.

I felt like an idiot scattering the catnip in the vacant lot. Then I hurried across to Moonjuice, letting myself in with my key.

I was in the "kitchen" area—a sink, a coffee urn, a paint-splotched table, a garbage can. I dumped the empty catnip boxes into the garbage. If anyone else had noticed the cats across the street, if anyone connected catnip to Moonjuice, I would point to these empties. I would make up some story. I didn't quite know what, but the main thing was to disassociate from Ygdrasil.

As soon as I dumped the boxes, I dashed through rows of folding chairs and ran up the stage steps.

The costumes were wildly tossed about, just as they'd been yesterday. But I couldn't find the fast-food worker uniform. I was afraid I knew why—because Georgia hadn't returned it to Moonjuice.

She must have gotten the Burger Burglar idea from seeing the uniform. Foolish!

"What's up?" Marlys had entered the room. She wore slacks and a mannish shirt and jacket, the uniform of her office day job.

I nearly screamed. "Oh, God, you scared me!"

"I noticed." She tossed her backpack down. "What happened here? Cyclone Georgia?"

"Yes."

She climbed the stage stairs. "It would never occur to her to clean up, that's for sure." Her tone was fond, not frazzled.

She started picking up dresses, putting them on hangers. She shook her head when the rough floor pulled a spangle off one.

"I'm surprised so many costumes are down here," she mused. "Shouldn't some of these be up in the attic? We're not using them this year are we?" She glanced at me. "I get a little sick of the hoo-haw dresses and boas. What next?" She struck a pose. "Joan Crawford and Judy Garland?"

"Right orientation, wrong gender," I commented.

I forced myself to calm down. I helped Marlys fold costumes and hang dresses. We talked about this year's show. She agreed with Georgia about the naked choir, which surprised me. She's usually pretty level-headed.

I didn't want to bring up the Burger Burglar or Cereal Killer or Catnip Kidnap, but I wished she would. I was looking for an excuse to let off steam, talk about it before the pressure blew my socks off. I even considered voicing my worry about Georgia. Marlys was both her friend and a reasonable person. She could counsel me, help me. She'd see the need to protect Georgia from her own excesses. And, as important, to protect Moonjuice from more scandal.

Marlys, work clothes and all, schlepped most of the costumes to the attic. I went into the tiny office area and switched on our most valuable resource, a laptop computer we'd purchased last year before our sponsors jumped ship.

I didn't have any work to do on it, but Marlys wouldn't know that. I wanted to stay longer than her. I wanted to search for evidence.

Marlys came down. She saw me at the laptop. "Book-keeping, poor baby?"

"Yes," I lied. I saw with annoyance that the computer battery was low. The adapter kept the juice on, but it wasn't recharging the battery. Either that or another board member had been using it.

"You have to do that now? I was thinking a mixed drink would taste good."

"No thanks." I was tempted, but I had something I wanted to do here. Alone. "Call Georgia?" I suggested.

"I've been trying her all afternoon. She's not home." She walked to the phone and dialed. A moment later, she smiled. Georgia had an outrageously campy telephone tape. "It's Marlys again, calling to see if you want dinner." She hung up, looking disappointed.

To me, she said, "You're sure you won't go play, Nan?"

"Sorry."

She shrugged, patting me on the shoulder before she left. I watched through the window as she tossed her pack into her old Honda, then drove away.

I ran up to the attic. A little guiltily, I reopened boxes Marlys had just neatly packed with costumes. I tried not to unfold any as I looked through.

I finally found the fast-food uniform at the bottom of a box in the corner. It wasn't one of the newly repacked boxes toward the front.

Georgia must have noticed the costume during yesterday's mess-spree, then thought of a clever way to use it. She must have brought it back sometime today and packed it away. It would, of course, never have occurred to her to put away the other costumes. That's what she had me and Marlys and a dozen other women with crushes on her for.

It was irritating. But I couldn't risk what she was willing to risk. I wouldn't feel safe until the uniform was no longer here to incriminate her. I carried it back downstairs with me.

If anyone noticed the cats out back and checked for

catnip, they'd find my empty boxes of non-Ygdrasil brand. I'd say I'd noticed cats fighting and sprinkled catnip to pacify them.

And no one would find the fast-food uniform at Moonjuice. I'd see to that right now. *

I turned off the laptop, turned out the lights, and carried the uniform away under my jacket. I drove to a beach cliff. I bundled the uniform into a tight ball, tying it with its own sleeves and pant legs. Then I dropped it off the cliff and went home.

I was watching the eleven o'clock news and eating ice cream when I learned disaster had struck anew.

A local computer company, the anchor informed me, a major manufacturer of laptop computers, had reported a break-in. Someone sneaked in and poured salt, pounds of regular table salt, all over the laptop battery assembly area. Thousands of dollars' worth of batteries had been ruined.

I waited for the anchor's inevitable statement. I was shocked when it didn't come. Maybe this one was too subtle for the folks at Channel 6. But someone would get it before tomorrow's paper rolled off the presses.

I would most certainly wake up to the headline SALT ON BATTERIES.

It was close enough to "assault and battery" to be Georgia's kind of pun. Georgia had struck again.

I guess performance art gets boring after a while. I guess it takes a criminal component to give art its edge.

I hardly slept at all that night.

I was a wreck the next day at work, barely following the convoluted ditziness of my students, barely jittering through a staff meeting, barely keeping my temper when the library accused me of damaging a book.

As soon as I could, I rushed to Moonjuice. Most of the

other board members were there. Georgia waved at me. She and two others were going through some papers. Georgia was laughing, saying, "Yes yes yes," as a woman named Marie insisted, "We can't put that into an ad!" Another woman, Heidi, was gushing, "Oh, Georgia's right! let's shake them up."

I didn't even want to know what kind of pornography Georgia was trying to sneak into a Moonjuice ad. She wore a lavender bodysuit with a silver sarong. The outfit had looked better on her when she was a blonde, but it was still eye-popping.

I went into the kitchen to pour myself some coffee before going in to join the wrangle.

Someone knocked at the back door. Usually people come in through the front.

I opened the door, alarmed to see a policeman.

"Hello." He smiled warily. This town has baggage about its treatment of lesbians and gays. The police have been trying to project a kinder, gentler image.

He carried a brown paper bag.

"What—? Who do you—? Hi." I had to calm down. He looked way too interested in my nervousness.

He showed me his ID. Then he waited, as if for me to blurt out some incrimination.

I knew, at that moment, that something had gone wrong. That he was here to question Georgia. That she'd been linked to the crimes. I wanted to box her ears for being so stupid.

"Do you mind if I come in?" the cop asked politely, as if I'd forget the Police Department's recent homophobia.

"No. What do you . . . ? Is there something?"

"Yes. I was hoping to speak to someone here? Anyone in charge?"

I didn't want him speaking to Georgia, that was for sure.

But there was something I very much needed to do right now, before he did any more snooping.

"I'll get Marlys," I said. "She's in charge. Kind of."

I dashed out of the kitchen, going straight into the office. I'd fetch Marlys in a minute. First, I was going to hide the laptop. I wanted no association in the cop's mind between Moonjuice and the salt on batteries.

I unplugged the laptop and kicked the power cord out of sight. I folded the screen down, and picked it up, brushing its dust outline off the desk. I turned with the laptop under my arm. I was going to stick it in the cupboard under some towels. Then I was going to hurry and get Marlys.

Instead, I stood there. Just stood there, holding the laptop.

The cop hadn't waited in the kitchen. He'd followed me.

Followed me! I wanted to crab, Don't you need a warrant? Don't you have any manners? But maybe it's police procedure to follow people so they don't go get shotguns or something. I wish I'd thought of that earlier. Marlys appeared in the doorway behind him.

I said, "I was just coming to get you. He wants to talk to you."

The cop had turned so he could keep an eye on us both. Georgia was coming toward us.

"I thought you two could talk in here," I said lamely. "I was just going to take the computer, and work in the kitchen."

Marlys, picking up on my freak-out, looked alarmed. Georgia strode into the middle of the situation like a bull into a china shop.

"Police?" She fiddled with her sarong as a child might. "We haven't even put our show on yet."

I was absolutely paralyzed. Georgia had the glitter-eyed look she gets before she flies into the ozone. Though I'd just said I was leaving with the laptop, I didn't.

The cop held up his paper bag. "We wondered if you could identify this for us."

I thought for a second he was going to pull out a gun, the one used to shoot Greg Purl's cereal. In retrospect, that might have been preferable.

He pulled out the fast-food uniform I'd tossed over the cliff last night. It looked damp and sandy.

"Our costume?" Georgia asked. "Is it?"

Marlys was frowning at her as if trying to warn her to be a little guarded for once.

The cop turned the collar inside out, showing the words "Moonjuice Gallery" in felt-tip marker.

Damn. Who'd been organized enough to do that?

I put the laptop back on the desk.

"I just labeled it!" Georgia exclaimed. "How funny! I did it because the overalls and ginghams disappeared."

I had to hand it to her, she was cool under fire. She smiled at me.

"I thought I'd get some brownie points from you, Nan. And I forgot to even mention it." She looked at me expectantly. "I did it two days ago."

"What a good idea," I said meekly.

"Well." She held out her hand for it. "Thanks for bringing it back." When he didn't return it, she looked confused. "I noticed a bunch of costumes were gone from the stage. I didn't realize they'd been stolen. I guess I thought Nan had one of her cleaning fits."

"I did," I told her. "We put them back in the attic."

"We think this may have been used in a burglary," the cop said. "Do you mind if I have a look around here?"

"Do you have a warrant?" Georgia said. She'd pulled herself to her full five feet ten inches. She looked regal. Rather, she looked like she was playing at looking regal.

"You object to me looking around?"

"No, of course not," Marlys interjected.

But Georgia elbowed her, saying, "Yes, we do. Without a warrant, you can't look around!" Her tone was adamant, and the look she shot Marlys clearly said, Shut up.

"Don't be silly, Georgia," Marlys insisted. "Why invite trouble? He just wants to look around. We don't have any secrets."

The cop glanced at the laptop I'd returned to the desk. He glanced at the fast-food uniform in his hand. He didn't look convinced we had nothing to hide.

And who knew what else Georgia had stashed here. Maybe even the gun.

"I agree with Georgia," I said. "As a matter of principle—"

"And history!" Georgia was on her high horse now. "We haven't forgotten Verboten." Verboten was a lesbian bar the cops had raided years ago, cracking heads and leading to the creation of a citizens' review board.

"Oh, you guys!" Marlys looked peeved. "You're making a mountain out of a molehill. We don't have anything to hide." She looked at me, clearly surprised. "Nan?"

But I repeated, "No. He should get a warrant if he wants to search. On principle."

I've never been so scared in my life. Not even Georgia's warm look of approval helped.

"Go!" Georgia said to the cop. "Go away. No warrant, no search." Still, the cop lingered. He caught Marlys's eye.

But Marlys looked at Georgia and knew she was licked. She said to the cop, "Where did you find the uniform, anyway?"

"Some tidepoolers brought it in."

Behind us, another board member—I hadn't seen her join us—said, "The Burger Burglar! You think he used our costume?"

Marlys, watching Georgia, looked ashen.

When the cop left, Georgia began prancing, repeating, "No warrant, no search; no warrant, no search." She treated us to a dazzling smile. "I've always wanted to say that."

"It was a damn stupid thing to say!" Marlys pushed past her, leaving the room.

"I wonder when they'll be back with the warrant," Georgia said. "Let's look around and make sure there's nobody else's business lying around for them to get into."

She went straight out of the room and up into the attic.

I could have hit myself with a hammer for doing that dumb thing with the laptop.

In the cop's mind, Moonjuice was connected to the burger burglary. Now my idiocy had reminded him of the salt on batteries, too.

I went into the kitchen. I had to get rid of the catnip boxes. They'd provide an additional associative link with the Catnip Kidnap. The boxes would be more incriminating than unincriminating now.

I pulled them out of the garbage. I went out the back door to put them into my car trunk.

I'd just closed the trunk when I turned to find the cop behind me.

"Do you mind if I ask you a few questions?" he said.

My heart sank.

"You know, I only came here to return the costume. Get some routine information." He stood too close. "But your attitude about this uniform, your behavior with the laptop computer, and now the catnip boxes." He shook his head. "Why don't you make it easy on everyone and talk to me."

But I'm the careful one, the practical one, the meticulous one. It's supposed to be Georgia who screws things up, not me.

"No," I said. "No, I can't."

I was so intimidated, I'd have confessed any of my own sins. But I couldn't deliver Georgia to the cops. This whole thing had been about protecting her.

I walked past him. I went back inside.

I'd ruined everything, I couldn't believe it. I'd put Georgia in peril of arrest. I'd undermined all our work at the gallery, and whatever reputation it still sustained.

I found Marlys sitting at the table.

"I've wrecked everything for Georgia," I confessed in agony. "They're going to investigate now."

"For Georgia?" she repeated. "Georgia's upstairs feeling important and dramatic." Marlys sounded almost bitter. "She'll be fine. She always is."

I tried to say more, but she waved me away. She didn't want to talk, that was apparent. I thought she must, in her heart, understand what I'd done to Georgia.

But I didn't fully understand the sparkle of tears in her eyes for three more days, until the cops came and made their arrest.

I should have known Georgia wasn't organized enough to pull off performance art crimes. I should have realized that Marlys was.

I should have realized Marlys wanted to feel she was more than just Georgia's friend, that she was also a kindred spirit. I should have recognized her need to distinguish herself from the rest of Georgia's entourage.

Marlys. If I'd known, I'd have trusted her to take care of things. I'd have butted out.

After the arrest, the story didn't get much press; Marlys

wasn't pretty enough to be a celebrity. Georgia was extravagant in her admiration, but only at first. Her attention span was too short to visit Marlys in jail. I thought Marlys would become a legend in the performance art community, but artists get depressed if they have to admire someone else.

By the time Georgia sang in the naked choir, nobody talked about poor Marlys anymore, that's for sure.

Dead Drunk

My secretary, Jan, asked if I'd seen the newspaper: another homeless man had frozen to death. I frowned up at her from my desk. Her tone said, *And you think you've got problems?*

My secretary is a paragon. I would not have a law practice without her. I would have something resembling my apartment, which looks like a college crash pad. But I have to cut Jan a lot of slack. She's got a big personality.

Not that she actually says anything. She doesn't have to, any more than earthquakes bother saying "shake shake."

"Froze?" I murmured. I shoved documents around the desk, knowing she wouldn't take the hint.

"Froze to death. This is the fourth one. They find them in the parks, frozen."

"It has been cold," I agreed.

"You really haven't been reading the papers!" Her eyes went on high-beam. "They're wet, that's why they freeze."

She sounded mad at me. Line forms on the right, behind my creditors.

"Must be the tule fog?" I guessed. I've never been sure what tule fog is. I didn't know if actual tules were required.

"You have been in your own little world lately. They've all been passed out drunk. Someone pours water on them while they lie there. It's been so cold they end up frozen to death."

I wondered if I could get away with, *How terrible.* Not that I didn't think it was terrible. But Jan picks at what I say, looking for hidden sarcasm.

She leaned closer, as titillated as I'd ever seen her. "And here's the kicker. They went and analyzed the water on the clothes. It's got no chlorine in it—it's not tap water. It's bottled water! Imagine that, Perrier or Evian or something. Can you imagine? Somebody going out with expensive bottled water on purpose to pour it over passed-out homeless men." Her long hair fell over her shoulders. With her big glasses and serious expression, she looked like the bread-baking natural foods mom that she was. "You know, it probably takes three or four bottles."

"What a murder weapon."

"It is murder." She sounded defensive. "Being wet drops the body temperature so low it kills them. In this cold, within hours."

"That's what I said.

"But you were . . . anyway, it is murder."

"I wonder if it has to do with the ordinance."

Our town had passed a no-camping ordinance that was supposed to chase the homeless out of town. If they couldn't sleep here, the theory went, they couldn't live here. But the city had too many parks to enforce the ban. What were cops supposed to do? Wake up everyone they encountered? Take them to jail and give them a warmer place to sleep?

"Of course it has to do with the ordinance! This is someone's way of saying, if you sleep here, you die here."

"Maybe it's a temperance thing. You know, don't drink."

"I know what temperance means." Jan could be touchy.

She could be a lot of things, including a fast typist willing to work cheap. "I just don't believe the heartlessness of it, do you?"

I had to be careful; I did believe the heartlessness of it. "It's uncondonable," I agreed.

Still she stooped over my desk. There was something else.

"The guy last night," Jan said bitterly, "was laid off by Hinder. Years ago, but even so."

Hinder was the corporation Jan had been fired from before I hired her.

She straightened. "I'm going to go give money to the guys outside."

"Who's outside?" Not my creditors?

"You are so oblivious, Linda! Homeless people, right downstairs. Regulars."

She was looking at me like I should know their names. I tried to look apologetic.

Ten minutes later, she buzzed me to say there was someone in the reception area. "He wants to know if you can fit him in."

That was our code for, *He looks legit.* We were not in the best neighborhood. We got our share of walk-ins with generalized grievances and a desire to vent at length and for free. For them, our code was, "I've told him you're busy."

"Okay."

A moment later, a kid—well, maybe young man, maybe even twenty-five or so—walked in. He was good-looking, well dressed, but too trendy, which is why he'd looked so young. He had the latest hairstyle, razored in places and long in others. He had shoes that looked like inflatable pools.

He said, "I think I need a good lawyer."

My glance strayed to my walls, where my diploma announced I'd gone to a night school. I had two years' experience, some of it with no caseload. I resisted the urge to say, *Let me refer you to one.*

Instead, I asked, "What's the nature of your problem?"

He sat on my client chair, checking it first. I guess it was clean enough.

"I think I'm going to be arrested." He glanced at me a little sheepishly, a little boastfully. "I said something kind of stupid last night."

If that were grounds, they'd arrest me, too.

"I was at the Club," a fancy bar downtown. "I got a little tanked. A little loose." He waggled his shoulders.

I waited. He sat forward. "Okay, I've got issues." His face said, *Who wouldn't?* "I work my butt off."

I waited some more.

"Well, it burns me. I have to work for my money. I don't get welfare, I don't get free meals and free medicine and a free place to live." He shifted on the chair. "I'm not saying kill them. But it's unfair I have to pay for them."

"For who?"

"The trolls, the bums."

I was beginning to get it. "What did you say in the bar?"

"That I bought out Costco's Perrier." He flushed to the roots of his chi-chi hair. "That I wish I'd thought of using it."

"On the four men?"

"I was high, okay?" He continued in a rush. "But then this morning, the cops come over." Tears sprang to his eyes. "They scared my mom. She took them out to see the water in the garage."

"You really did buy a lot of Perrier?"

"Just to drink! The police said they got a tip on their hot line. Someone at the bar told them about me. That's got to be it."

I nodded like I knew about the hot line.

"Now"—his voice quavered, "they've started talking to people where I work. Watch me get fired!"

Gee, buddy, then you'll qualify for free medical. "What would you like me to do for you, Mr. . . . ."

"Kyle Kelly." He didn't stick out his hand. "Are they going to arrest me or what? I think I need a lawyer."

★ ★ ★ ★ ★

My private investigator was pissed off at me. My last two clients hadn't paid me enough to cover his fees. It was my fault; I hadn't asked for enough in advance. Afterward, they'd stiffed me.

Now the PI was taking a hard line: he wouldn't work on this case until he got paid for the last two.

So I made a deal. I'd get his retainer from Kelly up front. I'd pay him for the investigation, but I'd do most of it myself. For every hour I investigated and he got paid, he'd knock an hour off what I owed him.

I wouldn't want the state bar to hear about the arrangement. But the parts that were on paper would look okay.

It meant I had a lot of work to do.

I started by driving to a park where two of the dead men were found. It was a chilly afternoon with the wind whipping off the plains, blowing dead leaves over footpaths and lawns.

I wandered, looking for the spots described in police reports. The trouble was, every half-bare bush near lawn and benches looked the same. And many were decorated with detritus: paper bags, liquor bottles, discarded clothing.

As I was leaving the park, I spotted two paramedics squatting beside an addled-looking man. His clothes were stiff with dirt, his face covered in thick gray stubble. He didn't look wet. If anything, I was shivering more than him.

I watched the younger of the two paramedics shake his head, scowling, while the older talked at some length to the man. The man nodded, kept on nodding. The older medic showed him a piece of paper. The man nodded some more. The younger one strode to an ambulance parked on a nearby fire trail. It was red on white with "4-12" stenciled on the side.

I knew from police reports that paramedics had been

called to pick up the frozen homeless men. Were they conducting an investigation of their own?

A minute later, the older medic joined his partner in the ambulance. It drove off.

The homeless man lay down, curling into a fetal position on the lawn, collar turned up against the wind.

I approached him cautiously. "Hi," I said. "Are you sick?"

"No!" He sat up again. "What's every damn body want to know if I'm sick for? 'Man down.' So what? What's a man got to be up about?"

He looked bleary-eyed. He reeked of alcohol and urine and musk. He was so potent, I almost lost my breakfast.

"I saw medics here talking to you. I thought you might be sick."

"Hassle, hassle." He waved me away. When I didn't leave, he rose. "Wake us up, make us sign papers."

"What kind of papers?'"

"Don't want to go to the hospital." His teeth were in terrible condition. I tried not to smell his breath. "Like I want yelling from the nurses, too."

"What do they yell at you about?"

"Cost them money, I'm costing everybody money. Yeah, well, maybe they should have thought of that before they put my-Johnny-self in the helicopter. Maybe they should have left me with the rest of the platoon."

He lurched away from me. I could see that one leg was shorter than the other.

I went back to my car. I was driving past a nearby sandwich shop when I saw ambulance 4-12 parked there. I pulled into the space behind it.

I went into the shop. The medics were sitting at a small table, looking bored. They were hard to miss in their cop-blue uniforms and utility belts hung with flashlights, scissors, tape, stethoscopes.

I walked up to them. "Hi," I said. "Do you mind if I talk to you for a minute?"

The younger one looked through me; no one's ever accused me of being pretty.

The older one said, "What about?"

"I'm representing a suspect in the . . ." I hated to call it what the papers were now calling it, but it was the best short-hand. "The Perrier murders. Of homeless men."

That got the younger man's attention. "We knew those guys," he said.

"My client didn't do it. But he could get arrested. Do you mind helping me out? Telling me a little about them?"

They glanced at each other. The younger man shrugged.

"We saw them all the time. Every time someone spotted them passed out and phone in a 'man down' call, we'd code-three it out to the park or the tracks or wherever."

The older paramedic gestured for me to sit. "Hard times out there. We've got a lot more regulars than we used to."

I sat down. The men, I noticed, were lingering over coffee. "I just saw you in the park."

"Lucky for everybody, my-Johnny-self was sober enough to AMA." The younger man looked irritated. " 'Against medical advice.' We get these calls all the time. Here we are a city's got gang wars going on, knifings, drive-bys, especially late at night; and we're diddling around with passed-out drunks who want to be left alone anyway."

The older man observed, "Ben's new, still a hot dog, wants every call to be the real deal."

"Yeah, well, what a waste of effort. Dirk," the younger man, Ben, shot back. "We get what? Two, three, four man-down calls a day. We have to respond to every one. It could be some poor diabetic, right, or a guy's had a heart attack. But you get out there, and it's some alcoholic. If he's too out of it to tell us he's just drunk, we have to transport and work him up. Which he doesn't want—he wakes up pissed off at having to hoof it back to the park. Or worse, with the new ordinance, he gets arrested."

"Ridiculous ordinance," the older medic interjected.

"And it's what, maybe five or six hundred dollars the company's out of pocket?" his partner continued. "Not to mention that everybody's time gets totally wasted and maybe somebody with a real emergency's out there waiting for us. Your grandmother could be dying of a heart attack while we play taxi. It's bullshit."

"It's all in a night's work, Ben," Dirk looked at me. "You start this job, you want every call to be for real. But you do it a few years, you get to know your regulars. Clusters of them near the liquor stores—you could draw concentric circles around each store and chart the man-down calls, truly. But what are you going to do? Somebody sees a man lying in the street or in the park, they've got to call, right? And if the poor bastard's too drunk to tell us he's fine, we can't just leave him. It's our license if we're wrong."

"They should change the protocols," Ben insisted. "If we know who they are, if we've run them in three, four, even ten times, we should be able to leave them to sleep it off."

Dirk said, "You'd get lawsuits."

"So these guys either stiff the company or welfare picks up the tab, meaning you and me pay the five hundred bucks. It offends logic."

"So you knew the men who froze." I tried to get back on track. "Did you pick them up when they died?"

"I went on one of the calls," Ben said defensively. "Worked him up."

"Sometimes with hypothermia," Dirk added, "body functions slow down so you can't really tell if they're dead till they warm up. So we'll spend, Oh God, an hour or more doing CPR. Till they're warm and dead."

"While people wait for an ambulance somewhere else," Ben repeated.

"You'll mellow out," Dirk promised. "For one thing, you see them year in, year out, you stop being such a hard-ass. Another thing, you get older, you feel more sympathy for how hard the streets got to be on the poor bones."

Ben's beeper went off. He immediately lifted it out of his utility belt, pressing a button and filling the air with static. A voice cut through: "Unit four-twelve, we have a possible shooting at Kins and Booten streets."

The paramedics jumped up, saying " 'Bye" and "Gotta go," as they strode past me and out the door. Ben, I noticed was smiling.

My next stop was just a few blocks away. It was a rundown stucco building that had recently been a garage, a factory, a cult church, a rehab center, a magic shop. Now it was one of the few homeless shelters in town. I thought the workers there might have known some of the dead men.

I was ushered in to see the director, a big woman with a bad complexion. When I handed her my card and told her my business, she looked annoyed.

"Pardon me, but your client sounds like a real shit."

"I don't know him well enough to judge," I admitted. "But he denies doing it, and I believe him. And if he didn't do it, he shouldn't get blamed. You'd agree with that?"

"Some days," she conceded. She motioned me to sit in a scarred chair opposite a folding-table desk. "Other days, tell the truth, I'd round up all the holier-than-thou jerks bitching about the cost of a place like this, and I'd shoot 'em. Christ, they act like we're running a luxury hotel here. Did you get a look around?"

I'd seen women and children and a few old men on folding chairs or duck-cloth cots. I hadn't seen any food.

"It's enough to get your goat," the director continued. "The smugness, the condemnation. And ironically, how many paychecks away from the street do you think most people are? One? Two?"

"Is that mostly who you see here? People who got laid off?"

She shrugged. "Maybe half. We get a lot of people who are frankly just too tweaked-out to work. What can you do? You can't take a screwdriver and fix them. No use blaming them for it."

"Did you know any of the men who got killed?"

She shook her head. "No, no. We don't take drinkers, we don't take anybody under the influence. We can't. Nobody would get any sleep, nobody would feel safe. Alcohol's a nasty drug, lowers inhibitions—you get too much attitude, too much noise. We can't deal with it here. We don't let in anybody we think's had a drink, and if we find alcohol, we kick the person out. It's that simple."

"What recourse do they have? Drinkers, I mean."

"Sleep outside. They want to sleep inside, they have to stay sober; no ifs, ands, or buts."

"The camping ban makes that illegal."

"Well," she said tartly, "it's not illegal to stay sober."

"You don't view it as an addiction?"

"There's AA meetings five times a night at three locations." She ran a hand through her already-disheveled hair. "I'm sorry, but it's a struggle scraping together money to take care of displaced families in this town. Then you've got to contend with people thinking you're running some kind of flophouse for drunks. Nobody's going to donate money for that."

I felt a twinge of pity. No room at the inn for alcoholics, and not much sympathy from paramedics. Now, someone—please God, not my client—was dousing them so they'd freeze to death.

With the director's permission. I wandered through the shelter. A young woman lay on a cot with a blanket over her legs. She was reading a paperback.

"Hi," I said. "I'm a lawyer. I'm working on the case of the homeless men who died in the parks recently. Do you know about it?"

She sat up. She looked like she could use a shower and a makeover, but she looked more together than most of the folks in there. She wasn't mumbling to herself, and she didn't look upset or afraid.

"Yup—big news here. And major topic on the street."

"Did you know any of the men?"

"I'll tell you what I've heard." She leaned forward. "It's a turf war."

"A turf war?"

"Who gets to sleep where, that kind of thing. A lot of crazies on the street, they get paranoid. They gang up on each other. Alumni from the closed-down mental hospitals. You'd be surprised." She pushed up her sleeve and showed me a scar. "One of them cut me."

"Do you know who's fighting whom?"

"Yes." Her eyes glittered. "Us women are killing off the men. They say we're out on the street for their pleasure, and we say, death to you, bozo."

I took a backward step, alarmed by the look on her face.

She showed me her scar again. "I carve a line for every one

I kill." She pulled a tin St. Christopher medal out from under her shirt. "I used to be a Catholic. But Clint Eastwood is my god now."

I pulled into a parking lot with four ambulances parked in a row. A sign on a two-story brick building read "Central Ambulance." I hoped they'd give me their records regarding the four men.

I smiled warmly at the front-office secretary. When I explained what I wanted, she handed me a records-request form. "We'll contact you within five business days regarding the status of your request."

If my client got booked, I could subpoena the records. So I might unfortunately, have them before anyone even read this form.

As I sat there filling it out, a thin boy in a paramedic uniform strolled in. He wore his medic's bill cap backward. His utility belt was hung with twice the gadgets of the two men I'd talked to earlier. Something resembling a big rubber band dangled from his back pocket. I supposed it was a tourniquet, but on him it gave the impression of a slingshot.

He glanced at me curiously. He said, "Howdy, Mary," to the secretary.

She didn't look glad to see him. "What now?"

"Is Karl in?"

"No. What's so important?"

"I was thinking instead of just using the HEPA filters, if we—"

"Save it. I'm busy."

I shot a sympathetic look. I know how it feels to be bullied by a secretary.

I handed her my request and walked out behind the spurned paramedic.

I was surprised to see him climb into a cheap Geo car. He was in uniform. I'd assumed he was working.

All four men had been discovered in the morning. It had probably taken them most of the night to freeze to death; they'd been picked up by ambulance in the wee hours. Maybe this kid could tell me who'd worked those shifts.

I tapped at his passenger window. He didn't hesitate to lean across and open the door. He looked alert and happy, like a curious puppy.

"Hi," I said, "I was wondering if you could tell me about your shifts? I was going to ask the secretary, but she's not very . . . friendly."

He nodded as if her unfriendliness were a fact of life, nothing to take personally. "Come on in. What do you want to know?" Then, more suspiciously, "You're not a lawyer?"

I climbed in quickly. "Well, yes, but—"

"Oh, man. You know, we do the very best we can." He whipped off his cap, rubbing his crewcut in apparent annoyance. "We give a hundred and ten percent."

I suddenly placed his concern. "No, no, it's not about medical malpractice, I swear."

He continued scowling at me.

"I represent a young man who's been falsely accused of—"

"You're not here about malpractice?"

"No, I'm not."

"Because that's such a crock." He flushed. "We work our butts off. Twelve hour shifts, noon to midnight, and a lot of times we get force-manned onto a second shift. If someone calls in sick or has to go out of service because they got bled all over or punched out, someone's got to hold over. When hell's a-poppin' with the gangs, we've got guys working forty-eights or even seventy-twos." He shook his head. "It's just plain unfair to blame us for everything that goes wrong. Field

124

medicine's like combat conditions. We don't have everything all clean and handy like they do at the hospital."

"I can imagine. So you work—"

"And it's not like we're doing it for the money! Starting pay's eight-fifty an hour; it takes years to work up to twelve. Your garbage collector earns more than we do."

I was a little off balance. "Your shifts—"

"Because half our calls, nobody pays the bill—Central Ambulance's probably the biggest pro bono business in town. So we get stuck at eight-fifty an hour. For risking AIDS, hepatitis, TB."\

I didn't want to get pulled into his grievances. "You work twelve-hour shifts? Set shifts?"

"Rotating. Sometimes you work the day half, sometimes the night half."

Rotating—I'd need schedules and rosters. "The guys who work midnight to noon, do they get most of the drunks?"

He shrugged. "Not necessarily. We've got 'em passing out all day long. It's never too early for an alcoholic to drink." He looked bitter. "I had one in the family," he complained. "I should know."

"Do you know who picked up the four men who froze to death?"

His eyes grew steely. "I'm not going to talk about the other guys. You'll have to ask the company." He started the car.

I contemplated trying another question, but he was already shifting into gear. I thanked him and got out. As I closed the door, I noticed a bag in back with a Garry's Liquors logo. Maybe the medic had something in common with the four dead men.

But it wasn't just drinking that got those men into trouble. It was not having a home to pass out in.

★ ★ ★ ★ ★

I stood at the spot where police had found the fourth body. It was a small neighborhood park.

Just after sunrise, an early jogger had phoned 911 from his cell phone. A man had been lying under a hedge. He'd looked dead. He'd looked wet.

The police had arrived first, then firemen, who'd taken a stab at resuscitating him. Then paramedics had arrived to work him up and transport him to the hospital where he was pronounced dead. I knew that much from today's newspaper.

I found a squashed area of grass where I supposed the dead man had lain yesterday. I could see pocks and scuffs where workboots had tramped. I snooped around. Hanging from a bush was a rubber tourniquet. A paramedic must have squatted with his back against the shrubbery.

Flung deeper into the brush was a bottle of whiskey. Had the police missed it? Not considered it evidence? Or had it been discarded since?

I stared at it, wondering. If victim number four hadn't already been pass-out drunk, maybe someone helped him along.

I stopped by Parsifal MiniMart, the liquor store nearest the park. If anyone knew the dead man, it would be the proprietor.

He nodded. "Yup. I knew every one of those four. What kills me is the papers act like they were nobodies, like that's what 'alcoholic' means." He was a tall, red-faced man, given to karate-chop gestures. "Well, they were pretty good guys. Not mean, not full of shit, just regular guys. Buddy was a little"—he wiggled his hand—"not right in the head, heard voices and all that, but not violent that I ever saw. Mitch was a good guy. One of those jocks who's a hero as a kid but then gets hooked on the booze. I'll tell ya, I wish I could have made

126

every kid comes in here for beer spend the day with Mitch. Donnie and Bill were . . . how can I put this without sounding like a racist? You know, a lot of older black guys are hooked on something . . . Check out the neighborhood. You'll see groups of them talking jive and keeping the curbs warm."

Something had been troubling me. Perhaps this was the person to ask. "Why didn't they wake up when the cold water hit them?"

The proprietor laughed. "Those guys? If I had to guess, I'd say their blood alcohol was one-point-oh even when they weren't drinking, just naturally from living the life. Get enough Thunderbird in them, and you're talking practically a coma." He shook his head. "They were just drunks; I know we're not talking about killing Mozart here. But the attitude behind what happened—man, it's cold. Perrier, too. That really tells you something."

"I heard there was no chlorine in the water. I don't think they've confirmed a particular brand of water."

"I just saw on the news they arrested some kid looks like a fruit, one of those hairstyles." The proprietor shrugged. "He had a bunch of Perrier. Cases of it from a discount place—I guess he didn't want to pay full price. Guess it wasn't even worth a buck a bottle to him to freeze a drunk."

Damn, they'd arrested Kyle Kelly. Already.

"You don't know anything about a turf war, do you?" It was worth a shot. "Among the homeless?"

"Sure." He grinned. "The drunk sharks and the rummy jets." He whistled the opening notes of *West Side Story.*

I got tied up in traffic. It was an hour later by the time I walked into the police station. My client was in an interrogation room by himself. When I walked in, he was crying.

"I told them I didn't do it." He wiped tears as if they were an embarrassing surprise. "But I was getting so tongue-tied. I told them I wanted to wait for you."

"I didn't think they'd arrest you, especially not so fast," I said. "You did exactly right, asking for me. I just wish I'd gotten here sooner. I wish I'd been in my office when you called."

He looked like he wished I had, too.

"All this over a bunch of bums," he marveled. "All the crime in this town, and they get hard-ons over winos!"

I didn't remind him that his own drunken bragging had landed him here. But I hope it occurred to him later.

I was surrounded by reporters when I left the police station. They looked at me like my client had taken bites out of their children.

"Mr. Kelly is a very young person who regrets what alcohol made him say one evening. He bears no one any ill will, least of all the dead men, whom he never even met." I repeated some variation of this over and over as I battled my way to my car.

Meanwhile, their questions shed harsh light on my client's bragfest at the Club.

"Is it true he boasted about kicking homeless men and women?" "Is it true he said if homeless women didn't smell so bad, at least they'd be usable?" "Did he say three bottles of Perrier is enough, but four's more certain?" "Does he admit saying he was going to keep doing it till he ran out of Perrier?" "Is it true he once set a homeless man on fire?"

Some of the questions were just questions: "Why Perrier?" "Is it a statement?" "Why did he buy it in bulk?" "Is this his first arrest?" "Does he have a sealed juvenile record?"

I could understand why police had jumped at the chance to make an arrest. Reporters must have been driving them crazy.

After flustering me and making me feel like a laryngitic parrot, they finally let me through. I locked myself into my car and drove gratefully away. Traffic was good. It only took me half an hour to get back to the office.

I found the paramedic with the Geo parked in front. He jumped out of his car. "I just saw you on TV."

"What brings you here?"

"Well, I semi-volunteered, for the company newsletter. I mean, we picked up those guys a few times. It'd be good to put something into an article." He looked like one of those black-and-white sitcom kids. Opie or Timmy or someone. "I didn't quite believe you, before, about the malpractice. I'm sorry I was rude."

"You weren't rude."

"I just wasn't sure you weren't after us. Everybody's always checking up on everything we do. The nurses, the docs, our supervisors, other medics. Every patient care report gets looked at by four people. Our radio calls get monitored. Everybody jumps in our shit for every little thing."

I didn't have time to be Studs Terkel. "I'm sorry, I can't discuss my case with you."

"But I heard you say on TV your guy's innocent. You're going to get him off, right?" He gazed at me with a confidence I couldn't understand.

"Is that what you came here to ask?"

"It's just we knew those guys. I thought for the newsletter, if I wrote something . . ." He flushed. "Do you need information? You know, general stuff from a medical point of view?"

I couldn't figure him out. Why this need to keep talking to me about it? It was his day off; didn't he have a life?

But I *had* been wondering: "Why exactly do you carry those tourniquets? What do you do with them?"

He looked surprised. "We tie them around the arm to

make a vein pop up. So we can start an intravenous line."

I glanced up at my office window, checking whether Jan had left. It was late, there were no more workers spilling out of buildings. A few derelicts lounged in doorways. I wondered if they felt safer tonight because someone had been arrested. With so many dangers on the street, I doubted it.

"Why would a tourniquet be in the bushes where the last man was picked up?" I hugged my briefcase. "I assumed a medic dropped it, but you wouldn't start an intravenous line on a dead person, would you?"

"We don't do field pronouncements—pronounce them dead, I mean—in hypothermia cases. We leave that to the doc." He looked proud of himself, like he'd passed the pop quiz. "They're not dead till they're warm and dead."

"But why start an IV in this situation?"

"Get meds into them. If the protocols say to, we'll run a line even if we think they're deader than Elvis." He shrugged. "They warm up faster, too."

"What warms them up? What do you drip into them?"

"Epinephrine, atropine, normal saline. We put the saline bag on the dash to heat it as we drive—if we know we have a hypothermic patient."

"You have water in the units?"

"Of course."

"Special water?"

"Saline and distilled."

"Do you know a medic named Ben?"

He hesitated before nodding.

"Do you think he has a bad attitude about the homeless?"

"No more than you would," he protested. "We're the ones who have to smell them, have to handle them when they've been marinating in feces and urine and vomit. Plus they get combative at a certain stage. You do this disgusting waltz with them where they're trying to beat on you. And the smell is like, whoa. Plus if they scratch you, you can't help but be paranoid what they might infect you with."

"Ben said they cost your company money."

"They cost you and me money."

The look on his face scared me. Money's a big deal when you don't make enough of it.

I started past him.

He grabbed my arm. "Everything's breaking down." His tone was plaintive. "You realize that? Our whole society's breaking down. Everybody sees it—the homeless, the gangs, the diseases—but they don't have to deal with the physical results. They don't have to put their hands right on it, get all bloody and dirty with it, get infected by it."

"Let go!" I imagined being helpless and disoriented, a drunk at the mercy of a fed-up medic.

"And we don't get any credit"—he sounded angry now—"we just get checked up on." He gripped my arm tighter. Again I searched my office window, hoping Jan was still working, that I wasn't alone. But the office was dark.

A voice behind me said. "What you doin' to the lady, man?"

I turned to see a stubble-chinned black man in layers of rancid clothes. He'd stepped out of a recessed doorway. Even from here, I could smell alcohol.

"You let that lady go. You hear me?" He moved closer.

The medic's grip loosened.

The man might be drunk, but he was big. And he didn't look like he was kidding.

I jerked my arm free, backing toward him.

He said. "You're Jan's boss, aren't ya?"

"Yes." For the thousandth time, I thanked God for Jan.

This must be one of the men she'd mother-henned this morning. "Thank you."

To the medic, I said. "The police won't be able to hold my client long. They've got to show motive and opportunity and no alibi on four different nights. I don't think they'll be able to do it. They were just feeling pressured to arrest someone. Just placating the media."

The paramedic stared behind me. I could smell the other man. I never thought I'd find the reek of liquor reassuring. "Isn't that what your buddies sent you to find out? Whether they could rest easy, or if they'd screwed over an innocent person?"

The medic pulled his bill cap off, buffing his head with his wrist.

"Or maybe you decided on your own to come here. Your coworkers probably have sense enough to keep quiet and keep out of it. But you don't." He was young and enthusiastic, too much so, perhaps. "Well, you can tell Ben and the others not to worry about Kyle Kelly. His reputation's ruined for as long as people remember the name—which probably isn't long enough to teach him a lesson. But there's not enough evidence against him. He won't end up in jail because of you."

"Are you accusing *us* . . . ?" He looked more thrilled than shocked.

"Of dousing the men so you didn't have to keep picking them up? So you could respond to more important calls? Yes, I am."

"But who are you going to—? What are you going to do?"

"I don't have a shred of proof to offer the police," I realized. "And I'm sure you guys will close ranks, won't give each other away. I'm sure the others will make you stop 'helping,' make you keep your mouth shut."

I thought about the dead men; "pretty good guys," according to the MiniMart proprietor. I thought about my-Johnny-self, the war veteran I'd spoken to this morning.

I wanted to slap this kid. Just to do *something*. "You know what? You need to be confronted with your arrogance, just like Kyle Kelly was. You need to see what other people think of you. You need to see some of your older, wiser coworkers look at you with disgust on their faces. You need your boss to rake you over the coals. You need to read what the papers have to say about you."

I could imagine headlines that sounded like movie billboards: "Dr. Death." "Central Hearse."

He winced. He'd done the profession no favor.

"So you can bet I'll tell the police what I think," I promised. "You can bet I'll try to get you fired, you and Ben and whoever else was involved. Even if there isn't enough evidence to arrest you."

He took a cautious step toward his car. "I didn't admit anything." He pointed to the other man. "Did you hear me admit anything?"

"And I'm sure your lawyer will tell you not to." If he could find a halfway decent one on his salary. "Now, if you'll excuse me, I have a lot of work to do."

I turned to the man behind me. "Would you mind walking me in to my office?" I had some cash inside. He needed it more than I did.

"Lead the way, little lady." His eyes were jaundiced yellow, but they were bright. I was glad he didn't look sick.

I prayed he wouldn't need an ambulance anytime soon.

If It Can't Be True

She regained consciousness seconds before the helicopter crashed. Gauges and instruments hurtled from one side of the claustrophobically small space to the other. Someone in the front was shrieking a panicked tone poem. Paraphernalia—stethoscopes, medicine bottles, clamps—hit her with the force of pinballs in a machine gone mad. An oxygen mask over her nose and mouth offered little protection.

She surfed a wave of dread, realizing this had happened to her before. She prayed it was just a bad dream this time.

When next she opened her eyes, she was still inside the helicopter but it was no longer in motion. A sheet of crushed laminated glass, glaring like glitter on glue, dazzled her. She was on her side, tipped toward the cockpit, the gurney wedged and buckled. A woman—a flight nurse?—was trapped beneath the gurney, her uniform soaked with blood. The nurse looked dead, red and wet like supermarket meat.

She supposed her own survival was a testament to good packaging and the tensile strength of the gurney. The plastic mask cut into her face, still feeding her oxygen.

Despite the fact that the gurney had twisted, the wrist-bands held. She jerked at them. Last time this happened, she'd been seat-belted like a passenger, not strapped down like an animal.

She could hear wind whistling through gashes in the metal sides of the helicopter. The crumpled windshield ballooned toward her, spilling bits of safety glass from its sticky laminate.

She wrenched her hands through the restrains, scraping off skin. It felt like a grease burn, shocking and scalding, but a monstrous dose of adrenaline helped her ignore it. She pulled free.

She couldn't remember what had put her into the helicopter, which she assumed to be a medical transport. It wasn't the airplane crash, that was a long time ago. She'd been a child then, they'd taken her to a foreign hospital where none of the nurses spoke English.

But whatever had put her here now, all she cared about was getting out. The door through which her gurney had been loaded was blocked, smashed against rocky ground. She crawled toward the cockpit, hoping for an exit there. But the window openings were flattened to slits. Broken tree limbs poked through parts of the metal. A branch no thicker than her thumb had skewered the pilot's body. She could see a second nurse's arm and shoulder, jagged bones poking through the skin.

She forced her attention away from them. She had to escape this grave of bloody flesh. There was a gash in the side, now the top, of the copter, maybe big enough to squeeze through.

She began squirming toward it. Her mask pulled off, and she could smell mud and pines and fried wires. As she hoisted herself out, frayed metal raked her clothes. She was surprised to see she wore a jumpsuit. Institutional clothes? She had a vague memory of locked doors and a tiny, unornamented room.

When she made it to the ground, she lay there panting, surrounded by splintered firs and scattered shards. A few minutes later, in horror of what had happened, she crawled a little farther away. And then a little farther still.

Drops of water from condensation on pine needles fell like light rain. Limbs creaked and rustled in a cold wind. The helicopter settled and shifted with deep groans that sounded like dirges.

She listened, watching the swaying evergreen pattern of branches against a gray and white sky. She must have been injured even before the crash; she wouldn't have been in a medical helicopter if not. But she couldn't put her finger on how it had happened or even what kind of injury.

She had the notion, as she paused there, that she'd chosen to let her memories go. Or worse, that she'd jumped away from them as if leaping from sweat-soaked sheets in the middle of a nightmare.

Memories were strange creatures, anyway, sliding deeper into dark crevices even as they lured you with bright hints and teasers. She'd been thinking a lot about memories. But, ironically, she couldn't remember why.

Well, someone was bound to come for her soon. Then she would learn what had happened to her, like it or not.

She closed her eyes. And a memory bloomed: Her brother, George, was saying, "Either we've both gone crazy or reality is stranger than we ever dreamed."

He was squatting beside a dead cow at the time. He was only fifteen years old, in work boots and a flannel shirt. She was eleven, standing behind him clutching his shoulder. The dead cow had been part of their father's herd.

In life, the cow had been as dumb and clumsy and easily prodded as others on the ranch. It had become remarkable only in death, resting in a shallow indentation in the hard ground. The flesh on the right side of its jawbone had been bloodlessly and completely sliced (or maybe lasered) away. Its right eye had been removed, leaving a perfectly clean white socket. Its anus had been reamed out. And where the udder should have been, there was only a hole as precisely oval as a puzzle piece. And there wasn't a drop of blood on the ground. Not a drop.

She and George would later learn there was no blood inside the cow either. And that the cow's ovaries had been neatly extracted with its colon and anus. No flies had buzzed around the carrion. And nothing, not even an indiscriminate rodent, had taken tooth to it.

Their parents had been away in town for the weekend. So George had phoned the neighbors, he'd taken pictures, he'd called the sheriff. And he and his sister had learned an interesting lesson at a young age. When faced with the incredible, people chose to settle for any explanation they could persuade themselves made sense.

Shown the cow, their neighbors suddenly accepted the notion of cults. Or they said it must be predators, even though they knew predators didn't make clean cuts or surgically remove ovaries. People refused to listen by turning off their heads as well as their ears. As one neighbor put it, "If it can't be true, it isn't."

Maybe she'd been lucky to learn life's most important lesson at the age of eleven, standing behind her brother, George. She learned that reality is no small and controllable thing, no mere doll house of familiar props. She was changed forever in one instant, diverted from the mainstream and splashed into another river altogether.

A voice said, "Aw, no—she's dead!"

She opened her eyes, never happier to prove someone wrong. She expected to find a man standing over her. She was trying to smile up at him as she opened her eyes.

But there was nothing above her but tree limbs against a

gloomy sky darkening toward nightfall.

She lifted her head. She had crawled into the brush, and greenery partly blocked her view. But she could see the commotion near the helicopter. She could see men silhouetted against its white paint. One was doubled over as if retching. He was being helped, practically dragged, away.

One of the remaining men reached into his jacket and pulled out a walkie-talkie. He clomped off without looking over his shoulder, without noticing her there on the ground.

The men had seen the pilot, the woman in front with him, and the one in back. Did they assume there was only one nurse on board? The nurse beneath the gurney, her uniform was obscured by blood. Maybe they thought she was the patient. Maybe they weren't searching for survivors because they supposed everyone was accounted for. She was about to call out, to tell them she was here, still alive.

But she heard someone say, "You think she brought the helicopter down?"

Another man said, "You believe all that bullshit?" Then, "Look at the sky, look at those clouds. It was a lightning bolt, has to have been." But he didn't sound convinced.

"All I meant was, maybe she got free and attacked the pilot."

"We told them to sedate her and restrain the hell out of her." The other man sounded angry. "God damn it, if we lose anybody . . . They should have stalled long enough for us to drive her."

"But how could something like this happen?" the first man persisted. "She must have gotten loose and done something."

Her hail died on her lips. These men seemed to blame her for the helicopter crash. What would they do to her if she announced herself?

She couldn't remember what she'd be going back to, but

she began to have a feeling it was something she didn't like. Maybe her jumpsuit was from some prison, maybe they'd been transporting her someplace worse. Maybe she was better off out here, wounded but free.

She lay still, her head raised, watching for them, trying to catch some telltale detail of conversation. But they were out of her range of sight now, and the wind brought only murmurs. Or perhaps they'd switched to a foreign language. She rested her head. The effort of keeping it up, of remaining watchful, had drained her of energy.

She closed her eyes and drifted away.

She jerked her head up again, achieving full wakefulness in an instant. Tree limbs swayed overhead, strobing the diminishing light.

She heard men's voices again but they were too distant to make out the words.

She'd been having nightmares about an institution where no one spoke her language, where she was corralled and regimented and never understood why—a ranch where she was just another dumb, nameless cow in the herd.

Hearing people run toward her, she rolled to her stomach and began to crawl for cover. She crawled farther from the wreckage, as far as she could on weak and pain-stiff limbs.

Acid boiled up her throat and seared her mouth but she didn't stop. She put as much distance as she could between herself and the helicopter.

She stopped when the men were close enough to hear her scrabbling. She sat behind a big tree, back against it, lacking the energy to crane her neck and see what these people were doing. She tried to quiet her breaths, calm her heartbeats, so she could hear them.

A man with a harsh accent said, "They're stringing him

along, but he's getting touchy. We don't have much time. Let's see if we can find *something* to help them out over there, any kind of proof what brought this baby down." The voice, gratingly defeatist, made her shudder. She'd heard it before somewhere, and the associations weren't pleasant. She heard boots scrunching on the duff. "You know what to do."

A few minutes later, she heard commotion and shouting. There was a huge roar as fire exploded upward with a sucking noise punctuated by booms. Had they started the fire on purpose? Turned up the flow of the oxygen canisters? Punched holes in the gas tanks? Doused the wreck with rocket fuel?

With her back to the helicopter, she could see the shadows of trees and branches dancing in hot light. She looked out from behind the tree. The fire was a huge plume of red and orange tumbling with black clouds of smoke. It sent off waves of heat and chokingly acrid smoke.

She got to her feet. If the fire spread, it would move faster than she could run. She knew that about fires, maybe learned it from someone. From George?

She tried to console herself with memories of her brother. She could feel the warm flannel of his shirt as she gripped him, looking down at their dead cow. The feel of his shoulder had provided reassurance. She needed that now.

She walked haltingly, painfully, as quickly as she could under the circumstances. She wound down a wooded ravine, away from the flaming debris of the helicopter that had brought her this far. She tried to take comfort in her homey memory of her brother, though it was spoiled by its association with the cow.

A few times, she had watched her father shoot cows. They would look startled, eyes opening wide and heads jerking back. Then they'd drop onto their front knees, pause infinitesimally, and keel over.

People killed each other pretty much the same way, she guessed. A stranger might kill you without anger, *blam,* for some reason or purpose of his own you would never understand.

As if you were a cow. Cows wouldn't understand being slaughtered for their meat because they didn't eat meat themselves. And as for being drained of blood and having their viscera pillaged, they could have no clue. That was beyond the understanding of any earthling, human or bovine.

She heard voices again—men moving closer. Hearing them through an inadequate curtain of redwood shoots, she tried to move faster. The men were bound to spot her soon. They might grab her and kill her—she had no reason to trust them. She needed more time, time to remember who she'd become in the years after finding the cow.

She shook her head as if to shake loose memories, to jump past her image of the cow. Her present life, her best interests, seemed to fall away as she turned that event over and over in her mind.

The discovery of the cow had ruined everything. Her gruff and level-headed father, for all his Rotary and Kiwanis Club and Ranchers Association contacts, had been derided mercilessly for stating the obvious: that no predator, no cult, no disease could drain a cow completely and remove its organs with laser precision. And he'd been too stubborn to back down, to pretend it was covens or coyotes. Her mother had been so mortified by the snickering, the graffiti, and the sneers that she overdosed on tranquilizers—which further convinced the neighbors they were all crazy, the whole family. For months every outing had been punctuated with jibes, or worse, pity. Her father began to lash out at everyone, especially his children.

She stopped. For a millisecond, she'd almost had it. She'd

almost gotten to the heart of this. Her father had done something, and because of it she'd ended up here.

She could see movement in the brush. She knew she'd have to hurry, that she didn't have time to think about it now.

But wherever George might be, she silently saluted him for being right. Reality was indeed stranger than they ever dreamed.

The man holding the bomb was interrupted by the ringing of his cell phone. He answered. "Is she here?"

"George?"

George ran a hand through his greasy hair. He must look pretty bad after sweating in this building for ten solid hours.

"George?" The man's voice was calm with authority. "George, there's been a slight delay bringing your sister."

George wanted to hit the switch. He'd let himself grow expectant, almost optimistic. There had been a few minutes when he'd almost believed this man, almost believed they'd take Jane out of the hospital and fly her here—without incident. He had tried for almost six hours to believe it, in fact. God knew, he wanted to believe. It was better than the alternative.

"George, listen to me," the man said urgently. "We're bringing her, we really are. There's just been a delay."

"Did you fly her already?"

"Almost here, really. But remember I told you weather conditions aren't good? Electrical storms, lightning—we don't want to take any chances. Just a short delay, that's all."

The explosives strapped to George's torso made his skin ooze with perspiration. The itching was almost beyond enduring. But if he unstrapped the pack, they'd shoot him for sure. He knew they must have him in their sights. He knew they'd kill him even though he hadn't hurt the hostages, just herded them around and had his say, that's all. The hostages were lying behind him now, trussed up and silent except for some whimpering. They smelled rank after all these hours and no bathroom breaks, that was for sure. But so did he.

For the thousandth time, he considered ending it, just blowing up this plain wood box of a building—this pen—full of people. He didn't care about any of them. And he'd just about had his fill of berating them.

It hadn't occurred to him to bring Jane here, not at first. It was the negotiators who kept asking him what he wanted. He was ranting at the hostages when he got the idea. If they could fly Jane here, then he might be wrong, after all. The hostages might be right, they might deserve to live. If the negotiator could get Jane all the way up here from Los Angeles within, say, four or five hours, that would mean they'd flown her for sure. You couldn't drive it in that amount of time.

But the hours had ticked by. And now the man on the phone was stalling him. Lying to him to keep his finger off the detonator.

"You're driving her here, aren't you?"

"We wouldn't do that, George. We made you a promise," the negotiator said.

George pictured him as avuncular and gray-haired with a potbelly and broken veins in his cheeks. But that was only because he'd once had a foster father who looked like that. For all he knew, the negotiator was lean and tough and decked out in SWAT team black with a bulletproof vest, like in the movies. It was hard to picture something so Hollywood in a cow town like this.

"Because the whole point of me talking to you at all," George repeated, "is you proving to me I'm wrong. Because I'd rather be wrong, I want to be wrong. I've always wanted that."

"We understand," the man assured him again.

But they didn't understand about Jane. Just like the hostages squirming behind him didn't understand.

"I knew you wouldn't bring her," George said. "I knew you were just stalling."

"She'll be here anytime. You'll see your sister, George, I promise."

It had been a long time since George had seen Jane. She'd been in the hospital since she was twelve years old, since their mother killed herself and their father went on a rampage against them for finding the cow and ruining his life. George couldn't take it. He'd run away. Later, he'd been shipped off to foster families. But they wouldn't let Jane go with him; she was too tweaked after the beatings she took.

At first they hoped with the right treatment she would get over it. They couldn't see it was that unknown thing, whatever killed the cow, that Jane really dreaded. Their father's thrashings might have damaged her brain, but mostly she was afraid of being sucked into the sky and having her organs cut bloodlessly out of her, that's what George thought.

But he hadn't seen her in years. He couldn't bear to look at her tied to a bed.

"You should have had plenty of time to fly her here by now—weather's not that bad. You're just stalling," he repeated.

"There are electrical storms over the mountains," the negotiator insisted. "I'm serious. You can feel the static in the air, can't you?"

But the air felt damp and heavy, not dry and charged.

George caught his breath. "That's what you're going to blame when she crashes. Isn't it?"

"There won't be a crash, George."

"Yes there will." He sat down, slumping with exhaustion.

"There always is." He'd already told them what happened when they tried to fly Jane to a special home in Oregon. And what happened when they tried to fly her back to the first hospital. "Anything she flies in, it comes down. It has to do with the cow. Don't ask me how."

He knew it sounded crazy. God knew, he'd gotten used to sounding insane. And yet, proof was proof. Two airplanes had crashed with Jane aboard. The investigators settled on other reasons, of course. They found faulty wiring in the first plane and cited a collision with a flock of birds in the other. This time, apparently, they meant to blame some storm.

George had just thought—prayed—that maybe . . . maybe they would put Jane up in the sky this time, and she'd make it. That would mean the other times were just bad luck, just coincidence. That the cow—

Well, there was no getting around the cow. George had seen it with his own eyes. Over the years, he'd researched it. There'd been thousands of similar cases from Mexico to Canada, always unexplained because there's no guessing how a cow can end up half embedded in the ground without a drop of blood around it or inside it, with its organs lasered out so perfectly the cells remained intact on either side of the incision.

In California, the Cattleman's Association was suing the government for information after dozens of members found their cows eerily mutilated. The association president discovered a steer with its three-foot horn embedded in hardpan all the way to its head.

But here, the ranchers still laughed at George. It hadn't happened again, it hadn't happened to any of them. And so they had that luxury.

"Don't you get it?" George spoke into the cell phone, his finger on the detonator. "Don't you get it about reality?"

"Look, everything's all right, George, really. Your sister's on her way."

"No. No, she isn't." He wanted to weep, thinking about Jane crashing again. And this time, it was his fault. He'd put her up in the sky to try to prove to himself that it couldn't be true. When he knew damn well it was.

"We understand about your worries," the man continued, "based on her bad luck before. But everything's going to turn out fine this time. We made sure your sister's comfortable and sedated. We're just waiting on the weather, just a slight delay, George. For your sister's sake, because we know she's paranoid about flying. You can understand that."

The negotiator's voice was as soothing as Mr. Rogers'. Maybe he could tell George had reached the end of his tether. Maybe he knew George was just about to hit the button.

"You're idiots, all of you," George fumed. "It's no use sedating Jane. She's not paranoid. Every time she flies she gets knocked right out of the sky—what's delusional about that? She's got brain damage from our dad beating on her. She's got short-term memory deficit, she's basically stuck where she was at age twelve. And her language processing is all screwed up—she either can't understand or doesn't want to. That's why she's been in that hospital all these years. But she's not crazy."

Or if she was, she'd come by it honestly.

George felt his skin beneath the taped-on bomb itch as if it were on fire. He'd let himself be seduced by the idea of proving himself wrong. Of seeing Jane again. As if touching her, embracing her, could pull him back through all these hard years to the good times of childhood. His longing was natural. But he blamed these smug officers for exploiting it.

"George, listen to me," the negotiator said urgently. "We can put your sister on the phone. We've got her, I swear. Just give me a few minutes, you can talk to her."

"She wouldn't understand me." Sometimes she seemed to catch a few phrases, but usually she looked bewildered and scared by what she took to be senseless chatter.

"Well, you can hear your sister, whatever she says or whatever sounds she makes. You can hear her voice. She can hear yours. You'll know she's on the way, George."

But he knew better than to believe the man. They were clearly desperate now, knowing George would soon find out that Jane had crashed. And once that came out, they knew it would be over. George would realize he'd sacrificed his sister's life just to try one last time to stop believing. How could he live with that? Even if he wanted to live.

Despair enveloped him. He lied: "If you let me talk to Jane, I'll wait a little longer."

But he heard booted feet on the old-fashioned verandah porch of the barnlike building. They could hear his intentions in his voice, he supposed. Oh, well.

George had the satisfaction of blowing them up along with the rest of the people cowering and weeping at the Cattle Ranchers Association Hall.

In the split second it took George to hit the button, he wondered what statement the press would derive from this. And whether the beings who killed that cow would understand what he was really saying.

The men who grabbed Jane spoke a language she didn't know. Just like the doctors and nurses at the hospital, just like the nurses in the helicopter.

That's when Jane realized she'd understood the men who first found the helicopter.

But how could that be? She hadn't understood anyone in a very long time. Since she was a child. Since her father went mad and clubbed her. She had awakened in a hospital bed with bandages over her shaved head, and no one had spoken more than random words or phrases of English to her since. Not ever again. Never till today. Maybe the helicopter crash had jarred something right. Maybe she would get her language back.

She felt the horrible tension of renewed hope. She tried to speak, to beg these men not to fly her back to the hospital, to drive her, for all their sakes.

But as always when she made sounds, the response was shaking heads and looks of incomprehension.

The frustration threatened to lift the top of her head off. She couldn't seem to breathe, as if she'd gone too deep underwater and suddenly realized she might not get back up in time.

This must have been how George felt, bolting from home so many years ago. He must have felt like a cork shooting from the bottle, helpless against the built-up pressure. Later, he blamed himself for leaving her alone with her father. She hadn't understood his words, but she had understood his heart. She had tried to tell him she forgave him for running away. What else could he do?

He had tried so hard to make the neighbors accept the reality of the exsanguinated cow, accept that it had happened, that they had all seen it, that whatever it meant, it meant it for all of them. But the neighbors had laughed at them, sneered at them, turned their backs. The neighbors seemed to know instinctively that people who didn't believe such things, their families stayed together. Their mothers didn't kill themselves, their brothers didn't flee, their fathers didn't go on rampages. No, the neighbors had been smart enough to refuse to believe the unbelievable.

She hoped George had made peace with it somehow. That

he'd stopped thinking about it all the time, like she did. She just couldn't seem to hang on to newer memories.

Half walking, half dragged away by the men, Jane wished for the millionth time that she could stop believing what she'd seen. She wished she could choose to be normal, choose belatedly to close her eyes and close her mind and even close her heart if she had to. She would close anything, even the ability to understand. Even the ability to communicate.

She scanned the sky for a sign that she could still undo it all. But the sky looked as ordinary as ever.

Dream Lawyer

"Picture this: a cabin in the woods, a hideaway, practically no furniture, just a table and a cot. Nobody for miles around, just me and her. I'm trying to keep her from collapsing, she's crying so hard. Her tin god's up and turned on her.

"She's got a gun there on the table, and I'm not sure what she's thinking of doing with it. Maybe kill herself. So I'm keeping myself between her and it. I'm up real close to her. Even crying doesn't make her ugly, her skin's so fresh. Tell the truth, I'm trying not to get excited. Her shirt's as thin as dragonfly wings, she's all dressed up expecting him. She should be hiding from him, but all day she's been expecting him. She's been dreading him but hoping he'll come, hoping he's got some explanation she hasn't thought of. Except she knows he couldn't possibly explain it away. That's why she's tearing herself up crying.

"She's so beautiful with the light from the window on her hair. But she's talking crazy—what she's going to do now, how she's going to tell everybody. Forgetting the hold he has on her, on all of us, how protected he is and how cool.

"And then . . . in he comes. She shuts up right away, surprised and terrified. I can tell by how stiff she gets, she's hardly even breathing. She's too freaked out to say any more. That's when I notice him there. But he's not paying attention to me. He's looking her over—her crying, the dress-up clothes she has on—and you can see he's making something out of it.

"She looks around like she's going to try to run. Big mistake. He goes cold as a reptile—I've seen it happen to him before. And then he picks up the gun and shoots her right in the face. Just as cold as a snake.

"That was my first thought, that it wasn't the person I knew, it was some . . . life-form, something outside my understanding with its own rules of survival like cockroaches. Because how could he just aim her own gun at her and blow her head off? Without blinking, without a word? After all she meant to him.

"I'm just about dying of shock right there on my feet. Compared to her, I'm nobody to him, nothing, just a bug that rode in on his cuff. Maybe that's why he says, 'I won't kill you. I don't have to.' He starts walking out. At the door he turns. 'If I have to kill you later, I will. But not like this. By inches. You'll see it coming a long way off, Juan. You'll see it coming for miles, so don't look back.'

"That's all. He didn't try to explain anything or change her mind. He didn't say a word to her, not even good-bye. He just killed her like she didn't matter. Like she was a fly and he was a frog. Zap. And then he left.

"By then I could hardly even stand up. I could hardly make my feet move to look closer at her. I wish I never did look. Did you ever have a bee get squashed on your windshield? That's what her head looked like. I wouldn't have expected so many colors of . . . Her face was blown right off except one part where there were still curls caught in a hair clip.

"I could barely keep on my feet much less figure out what to do about it. It was clear she was dead. Or wouldn't want to be saved, if she wasn't. So it was no use calling nine-one-one.

"And as to him, well, my God, how was anybody going to believe me? With all his followers and his credentials—who's going to take my word over his? And what did he mean about don't look back? What would he do to me, this reptile-man who could blow away someone that loved him and that probably he loved, too. What would happen to me if I told anybody?

"I wish I could say I was confused over the trauma or something, but I was probably more scared than anything. That's why I left her there. I was too scared to do anything else, just too damn scared. Because I felt like I'd finally seen right inside him and found the devil there. I hit the road and stuck out my thumb, just trying to get some distance, trying to keep myself together.

"You probably know what happened after that. It took the police a while to catch up to him. They were looking for me, too; they knew I was there at the cabin from finding my fingerprints and hairs and like that. When they found me, I could hardly get any words out, I was still so scared. I guess they didn't trust me to stay and testify against him—they put me in custody, in jail. I wanted to get word to him, beg him not to do anything to me, beg him to understand it wasn't my fault, that I'd have shut up and stayed gone if I could. But I knew it was useless.

"When it was his lawyer's turn to do something, she had all these reasons I shouldn't testify. What it came down to was, I couldn't prove it was him and not me that killed Becky. I pointed at him and he pointed at me. And I guess in some legalistic way, we canceled each other out. However the technicalities worked, the jury never heard the whole story. So there was no way for them to figure out the truth, not beyond a reasonable doubt. I don't blame them the way some folks around here do.

"Some people wrote to the newspapers that they should have put me in prison whether I did it or not, because Becky was dead and somebody had to pay. And if it wasn't going to be Castle, it should be me because we were the only ones there in the cabin with her.

"And I can understand how people felt. It makes me sick to know he shot her and got away with it. And her, poor thing, all dressed up in case he was going to melt at her feet, hoping he'd come clean to everybody just to keep her respect. That's the part that hurts the most, that she was good enough to hope so even with what she knew about him.

"I'd have twisted my life inside out to please a sweet girl like Becky Walker. I cry every time I think about her beautiful gold hair caught in that little clip. I couldn't save her, and I couldn't even get her a little bit of justice. Not even that.

"I tell you, it tears me apart."

The poor man looked torn apart. His natural swarthiness had paled to a sickly yellow. His graying hair was disheveled from finger-raking. His dark eyes, close-set above a hooked nose, glinted with tears. Prominent cheekbones contributed to the starved, haunted look of a survivor.

The walls of his small house were cluttered, even encrusted, with charms of various types. Mexican-made saints cast sad eyes on dried herbs and wreaths of garlic, rusty horseshoes were strung with rabbits' feet, icons of saints hung beside posters of kindly blond space aliens. And everywhere there were gargoyles. Their demon faces scowled down from the rafters, they brooded in corners, squatted on tabletops, leered behind rows of votive candles.

"Did you have a lawyer representing you before or during the trial?" I asked Juan Gomez.

"No."

"When the police questioned you, did they tell you it was your right to have a lawyer present?"

"Yes." He buffed the knees of his worn jeans, rocking

slightly. "But what was the point? I was too scared to say what happened, anyway."

"But you feel you need a lawyer now?" Castle had been acquitted of murder: The barn door was open, and the horse was long gone. Unless Gomez wanted some pricey commiseration, there wasn't much I could do for him.

When he nodded, I continued. "I gather this was a big case locally. But I just moved here, so I'm not acquainted with it." Having been fired from yet another law firm, this time for taking a too-strange case as a favor to a friend, I was once again on my own. Just today, I'd unpacked a parcel of business cards reading "Willa Jansson, Attorney at Law, Civil Litigation & Criminal Defense." I wasn't turning down anything until I got a little money in the bank.

The move from San Francisco to Santa Cruz had been expensive despite being only seventy-five miles down the coast. And I'd discovered that lawyers in laid-back Hawaii East charged only half the fees of their big-city counterparts.

Now my potential client, whose main selection criterion seemed to be counsel's willingness to make house calls, leaned back in his chair. It was painted white, like the rest of his plain wood furniture, and arranged on duct tape exes on the floor.

"You never heard of the case? You don't know about Sean Castle?" He resumed his anxious rocking.

"No. The name seems familiar." Maybe I'd read about him.

"He's famous for dream research."

"Dream interpretation, that kind of thing?"

"Prophetic dreaming." He continued to look surprised I didn't know. "Sean could lecture seven days a week about dreams and never run out of people wanting more. There's a waiting list for his workshops. He's a brilliant man."

"What does he teach people to do?"

"Recognize the future in their dreams."

I shuddered at the thought. Bad enough to deal with the future when it got here. "What did the dead woman threaten him with? What was she going to expose about him?"

He jerked back as if I'd slapped him. "I can't tell you that."

"I'm sorry?"

"That was up to her." He winced. "It's still up to her. I can't take it away from her."

"But she's dead." Was I missing something?

"A carpet doesn't stop unrolling just because the ground drops out from under it."

"Well, but . . . I don't know where this carpet's going." I did know I'd gone as far as I could with the metaphor. "You say Castle killed her so she wouldn't reveal some secret. And now you feel vulnerable because of it. Maybe you should share the information, if only for your own protection."

"You don't know this because you never met him." Juan looked more than merely earnest. "He means what he says, especially threats."

"You're afraid he'll kill you?" At least that part made sense to me. "Or however he put it."

"I'm not 'afraid' he'll do it, I know he will. Exactly like he said. By inches. It's already started." He watched me glance at the gargoyles. "Gargoyles are demons that switched sides. Because of who they used to be, they can see through any disguise evil puts on—it takes one to know one. They keep evil from coming close, like pit bulls in the yard. That's why they're all over cathedrals."

I glanced uncertainly at the snarling plaster creatures, some winged, some with horns and claws. They were daunting, but pit bulls barked louder.

"You need them when you're sleeping," he added. "You can't stay awake forever."

"No." I continued hastily, "So why do you want a lawyer?" An exorcist, a shaman, a psychic, even an acupuncturist would probably be more useful for counteracting psychological terror. When he didn't respond, I said, "Look, I'm no therapist, but it does seem that Sean Castle is playing on your fears. Manipulating them."

"You'd have to meet him to understand. If he wants something, it happens."

"Okay. But do you need counsel?" He seemed unclear on the demarcation between legal remedies and mythical talismans. And I still had plenty of unpacking to do.

"The lawyer sent me his will."

"He's dead?" I wasn't going to learn Juan Gomez was afraid of a ghost?

"No, he's alive—I'm absolutely sure. So why did his lawyer send me the will? Why does she think *he* lives here? Why did he tell her that? What does it mean?"

"Who's the lawyer?"

"Laura Di Palma." He watched me. "You know her."

"Yes." I don't know what showed on my face. But Di Palma had once cross-examined me in a murder trial. She'd tied me into incoherent knots and invited the jury to scorn my testimony. The experience had been akin to being repeatedly stabbed with an icicle. There was a lingering chill long after the pain subsided. "She didn't explain why she sent the will here? Did she send a cover letter?"

"Just the will. The envelope has her return address."

"Are you named in the will?"

The mention of Di Palma made me more curious than cautious. We shouldn't be discussing this unless and until we agreed I was his lawyer and talked about fees.

"He wants me to take his ashes to Becky's cabin and scatter them there." He blanched just thinking about it.

"You can refuse."

"No, there's a reason he did this. He's trying to tell me something. More than that." He resumed his neurotic rocking. "He's trying to trap me, do something evil to me. I need to figure out what. I need you to talk to his lawyer for me."

"You want me to find out her reasons for sending the will to your address? Or his reasons for wanting you to scatter his ashes?"

"Find out anything, whatever he told her. But don't talk to him yourself." He leaned forward. "Don't put yourself in his line of sight. Don't let him know you're against him. Okay? I have enough on my conscience already."

"Don't worry about me." If I could survive another encounter with Laura Di Palma, I was tough enough to face a mere assassin.

"And her, the lawyer. Be careful of her. Everybody that touches him gets some of the good burned out."

"Di Palma doesn't give him much of a target." I hastened to recover some professionalism. "What I mean is, she can take care of herself."

"No." He shook his head emphatically. "Against him, nobody takes care. You've got to sleep sometime."

I suppressed a smile, imagining Di Palma wrestling with nightmares. If anybody could get a restraining order against Freddie Krueger, it was her. "Why don't you let me take a look at the will?"

He rose and walked to a white velvet box on a whitewashed table. From it he extracted a pair of latex gloves. He put them on, then carried the box over to me.

"Do you want gloves?" he asked. "I have more."

"No, that's okay." I reached into the box and pulled out a manila envelope. The return label was preprinted with Di Palma's law firm address. The envelope was addressed in tidy type to Sean Castle . . . at this address. In block letters above were the words "Juan Gomez" and "c/o," in care of. "It might just be misaddressed. A clerical error."

"I want to wish it could be so simple!"

I slid the will out. It looked like a Xerox or laser print of a standard-format will. I skimmed a page that distributed property and personal effects among a list of people, none with the surname Castle.

Juan's name appeared in a section about funeral arrangements and disposal of remains. It requested, without embellishment, that Juan take the urn containing Castle's cremains to "the mountain cabin formerly the residence of our mutual friend, Becky" and scatter them there.

I looked up from the will to find Juan standing as hunched and motionless as one of his gargoyles.

"Who owns the cabin he's talking about?" I asked him. "Are they going to want these ashes scattered there?"

"It used to be mine. But I deeded it to Sean so he could put Becky in it. She had to be isolated, and it's pretty far off the beaten path."

"Isolated?"

"That's what Sean said. Now I know what he meant, but then, I didn't think about it. She wanted to live there, so that was that."

"Did she realize it wasn't originally Castle's property? That you were deeding it to him for her benefit?"

He shrugged. "She knew I built it."

I hadn't been his lawyer then; this was none of my business. People signed property over to churches and foundations and gurus everyday. Scientologists bought enlightenment one expensive lesson at a time, Mormons tithed inconvenient percentages of their income, my father's favorite guru, Brother Mike, gladly accepted supercomputers.

"Who lives in the cabin now?"

"I don't know. I've never been back. I think of it as empty." He looked wistful. "If only . . . It could have worked out fine for everybody."

I waited, but he didn't elaborate. It certainly hadn't worked out well for the dead woman. Or, apparently, for Juan Gomez.

I returned my attention to the will, one of the first I'd studied since the bar exam. "Aside from being addressed to you care of Sean Castle, it's odd they'd send this out prior to Castle's death. You're sure he's still alive?"

"Yes. I wish he weren't, but I know he is."

"Well, it's not standard practice to distribute a living person's will, not at all. It raises beneficiaries' expectations, and that's unfair all around—the person might change his mind and revise the terms of the will or add a codicil. So I don't know why he'd want this mailed out now. It doesn't promise anything and it invades his privacy. It really might be some kind of mistake."

"He doesn't make mistakes."

"Neither does his lawyer. But a paralegal may have screwed up. Maybe the wrong address in the Rolodex or a misleading scrawl on a Post-it . . . these things do happen." Bad enough Juan had been asked to scatter a murderer's ashes. He shouldn't have to worry about the will containing some hidden threat. "I could find out for you."

"Yes! But be careful. You don't know Sean Castle, you don't know what he does to people."

But I did know Laura Di Palma. And Juan Gomez was a good example of what *she* did to people.

★ ★ ★ ★ ★

"Willa, it's been years." Di Palma's law partner stood in the waiting room of her office, looking mildly surprised. "Are you still practicing labor law?"

I felt a little guilty saying, "No." I'd gone to law school to join the labor firm of illustrious lefties Julian Warneke and Clement Kerrey. Maryanne More had apprenticed there years before me, going on to the National Labor Relations Board before starting her own firm. But I'd stayed with Julian only two years before the lure of solvency seduced me into an L.A. business firm. I'd done a year of hard time there—despite my efforts to reinvent myself, I'd remained a hippie at heart, valuing my time above money. From a labor point of view, I'd been one sullen wage slave. "I just opened my own firm. Down in Santa Cruz. I'd like to pick up a labor clientele, but I'm barely unpacked."

In fact, that was why I was here now. As long as I was in the city to fetch the last of my boxes, I might as well get in Di Palma's face.

Maryanne nodded. With her smooth chignon and velvet lapels, she looked like a model in a Christmas catalog. "Are you here to see me?"

I glanced at the waiting room's dark wood walls, brocade couches, and Old Master oil paintings. All the place needed was a docent. The decor sure didn't match my impression of Di Palma. I suppose I'd envisioned shark tanks.

"I've been trying to reach Laura Di Palma. I've left several voice-mail messages and I haven't gotten a response. I thought I'd drop in and see if I could catch her."

Maryanne seemed to stop breathing, tensing as if she were listening for something. "I'm sorry, Laura's taken the week off to take care of some family matters. Can I help you?"

"Possibly."

Maryanne nodded slightly, motioning me to follow her down a parquet corridor. Halfway down, a door labeled "Laura Di Palma" was ajar. In an office splashed with bright colors, a lanky man sat at a glass desk, holding his bowed head. Maryanne sped up, leading me to an office at the end of the hall.

I settled into a wing chair. Jeez, her office looked like a palace library.

"Laura Di Palma sent a copy of a will to Juan Gomez, my client. Among other things, the will asks him to scatter the ashes of her client, Sean Castle. The envelope is addressed to Juan at his house, care of Sean Castle."

Maryanne shook her head slightly. "How odd." Neither of us stated the obvious, that sending the will to someone named in it denied Castle the confidentiality he might reasonably expect. "I assume it was misaddressed, and that she intended to send it to . . . Sean Castle, is it? I'm sorry if your client was disturbed by it."

I sighed. "Disturbed is the least of it. Mr. Gomez worries that Castle gave Ms. Di Palma his address. And he particularly wanted to keep his whereabouts secret from Castle. So I really need to check with Ms. Di Palma and find out what's behind this."

"Well, I can't speak for her. But perhaps I can find out whether it was a clerical error." She looked bothered. Because the office might have to notify Castle? Because she shouldn't have to clean up Di Palma's mess?

"I'd like to talk to Ms. Di Palma myself. My client really needs some assurance that Mr. Castle's not making some kind of veiled threat." After the creepy tale Juan had told, I could use a little reassurance myself. "You know Juan Gomez testified against Castle?"

"I don't know anything about Mr. Gomez. And I really

don't know much about Mr. Castle, though I recall Laura represented him last year. But I'll ask her to—" She caught her breath, looking beyond me. "Sandy?" Her tone was bracing.

The lanky man I'd glimpsed in Di Palma's office was now standing in the doorway. A wide mouth and long dimples might ordinarily have been the focus of his thin face. But at this moment, gloom furrowed his brows and narrowed his blue eyes to a wince. He pushed sand-colored hair off his forehead, looking like Gary Cooper in some thirties melodrama.

"Did I hear you mention Laura?" His voice was deep and slightly Southern in inflection. "Anything I can help with?"

Maryanne glanced at me.

He continued standing there, so I said, "I've been trying to get hold of Ms. Di Palma."

The man entered, taking the wing chair beside mine. "About?"

"Sandy, I don't think this is—"

"What about?" he repeated.

"Are you an associate of hers?" I wondered.

"Willa Jansson, Sandy Arkelett. Sandy handles our private investigations." Maryanne's lips remained parted, as if she were on the brink of saying more.

I watched her uncertainly. Arkelett worked for her firm, this should be her call.

Finally, she told him, "Laura apparently sent Sean Castle's will to one of his beneficiaries."

Arkelett's brows rose.

"Juan Gomez. He's my client," I added. "He'd like to know why the will was sent to him. He and Mr. Castle were involved in a case she tried."

"I know Castle. I did the legwork on that case."

"Have you seen him lately? Do you know if the will was sent at his request?"

"Laura didn't tell me about any will." Arkelett was talking to Maryanne now. "You?"

Maryanne shook her head. ✎

"Could it be a phony?" He reached a long arm across the desk as if to take a copy from Maryanne.

"My client didn't want me to make a copy," I explained. I didn't add that he'd nearly come unglued at the prospect of my becoming cursed by it. "It looked like a standard document with a number of bequests. It asks my client to scatter Castle's ashes."

"And it got sent to . . . ?"

"Juan Gomez."

He scowled. "I'll try and get a hold of Castle for you. Do you have a business card?"

I was a little surprised. It would certainly be more usual to contact Di Palma, wherever she was, before going behind her back to question her clients. Nevertheless, I fished two brand new cards out of my bag, handing one to Arkelett and one to Maryanne.

"Law school murders," Arkelett said, reading my card. "You were one of the witnesses."

I felt myself trying to scoot back the heavy wing chair.

"I worked with Laura on that case," he explained.

As the defense investigator, he'd have done a thorough background check of the prosecution's witnesses. He'd have given Di Palma details of my protest-era arrests and my two ghastly months of jail time. God knew Di Palma had gotten her money's worth, rattling my "criminal record" like a saber, using it to hack away at my credibility.

But, as lawyers love to say, that's why she got the big bucks.

Arkelett slipped my card into his pocket, and rose. He left without another word.

Maryanne said, "We'll try to reach Laura for you, of course."

Then she rose, too, resolutely shaking my hand good-bye.

Arkelett stopped me in the hall outside the suite of offices.

"Look," he said, "I want to ask a favor. I'd like to see Castle's will. Maybe ask your client a couple of questions." He frowned. "Because Laura . . . it wouldn't be like her to screw up. Not on a client matter, anyway."

"What would the will tell you?" And why didn't he just phone Di Palma, wherever she was?

"If you still have the envelope, the date and place it was mailed."

"I could call you with the information."

"I want to look at it myself. In case there's anything else."

Was he expecting blood? A coded scrawl? Juan had made this all seem strange enough. Having a man in a business suit get weird about it was even spookier.

"Some things you need to look at the original," he insisted. "I'd just like to make my own assessment. Take a few minutes of your client's time?" He tilted his head as if to figure me out.

"I don't know—he's a little high-strung." I couldn't resist asking: "Is there a problem? Some reason you're not waiting for Ms. Di Palma?"

He chewed the inside of his cheek. "Laura had to go deal with a . . . a sick cousin." Judging by his face, there was a hell of a lot more to it than that. "And well, we're not sure exactly where that took her. I don't mean to say it's a big deal—she'll be back soon enough. But in the meantime, guaranteed, she'd want me to check this out."

Check out the postmark on Juan Gomez's envelope? No, however Arkelett might try to soft-pedal it, he wanted to know where Di Palma had gone. I backed toward the elevator. Should I help him? If Di Palma wanted him to know her whereabouts, she'd have told him herself.

"I can maybe help your client out," Arkelett persisted. "If he's who I think he is." He looked nonplused. "Maybe I can help him get his head on straight."

"My client's afraid," I admitted. "Afraid of Castle. He warned me about him several times. And he expressed some concern about Ms. Di Palma, too. So I don't know how he'd feel about seeing you."

Sandy Arkelett leaned closer. I could smell Old Spice on his lean cheeks. "If he wants you present, that's fine. No cost to him   I'll pay you for the hour, okay?"

"I'll see what I can set up." For a fee, I supposed I could fit it into my schedule.

When he opened his door, I said, "How are you, Juan? I'm sorry I'm a little early."

As I stepped in, he glanced outside, his grizzled brows rising. I looked over my shoulder. Sandy Arkelett had just pulled up to the curb.

Juan clutched his sweatshirt as if to keep his heart from leaping out of his chest. And I didn't blame him. Just as Arkelett had investigated me when I'd been a witness against Di Palma's client, he'd doubtless investigated every aspect of Juan's life before Castle's trial. I wondered how Juan would react if Arkelett alluded to any of it.

I closed the door.

"You don't have to do this," I reminded him. "Or, if you like, we can speak to Mr. Arkelett in my office. You don't have to invite him into your home."

"No." Juan's tone was more stoic than his face. "No, I understand what it is to love someone. Someone who's gone."

I'd told him Di Palma was apparently off on some private errand. I'd told him I thought Arkelett was trying to find out exactly where it had taken her. Now Juan had filled in the reason: Arkelett was in love with Di Palma. Maybe Juan was just guessing, but it fit, it made sense.

I looked around the gargoyle-protected room. It was somber with the curtains closed, lighted only with votive candles and a dim table lamp. He must not read much, not in this gloom. But there was no television in sight, either. Did he spend his days praying to the gargoyles leering in flickering candle shadows? "You've met Sandy Arkelett?"

Juan nodded. "He's by her side all the time. He puts himself between her and Castle. You can see that he understands more about Castle than she does. You can see it on his face."

I was a little taken aback. He couldn't have spent much time with Castle and his lawyer. Even his use of the present tense was disconcerting. He seemed to expect me to share some memory or vision.

Sandy Arkelett sighed deeply when Juan opened the door to him. It was a moment before he muttered, "Thanks for seeing me." The worry lines on his long face deepened, lending his words a somber sincerity. "Mind if I come in?"

I admired his thirties-movies silhouette, long and slim in a slightly baggy suit. Even his light brown hair was combed back like Gary Cooper's or Jimmy Stewart's. Di Palma was lucky.

"I was just asking my client if he felt comfortable doing this," I told him.

Juan was flattened against the door, staring at Arkelett.

The detective said, "I won't take but ten minutes of your time, Mr. um . . ." He eyed Juan so intently he seemed to be leaning toward him. "Is it Gomez?"

Juan edged away.

"I know I bring up some hard memories. So I'll make it real short," Arkelett repeated. "But it was a long drive down here—I'd appreciate ten minutes."

"I—I'm sorry. I have nothing against you. On the contrary. I just—"

Arkelett stepped quickly inside. "Thanks," he murmured. "I guess . . . would it be easiest to start with the will?" He glanced at me.

"Do you mind showing Mr. Arkelett the will?"

Juan caught his lower lip between his teeth. He walked to the white box on the white table. Arkelett looked around, his pale brows pinched. I watched Juan put on rubber gloves to open the box and handle the manila envelope inside it.

He brought it to me. Arkelett stepped up behind me, positioned to look over my shoulder.

The envelope was postmarked Hillsdale, CA. Central California, maybe Northern? Like most San Franciscans— former San Franciscans—I'd rarely bestirred myself to explore the outback.

I turned, handing Arkelett the envelope. It had been mailed on the sixteenth. Today was the Twenty-second.

Juan reached past me, touching his fingertips to Arkelett's elbow. "Sit down," he said. "On the white pine chair. That's the best one for this. Do you want gloves?"

"No need." Arkelett chewed the inside of his cheek and stared at the postmark.

"Where's Hillsdale?" I asked him.

"North." It seemed to take him extra effort to look away from the word. Then his head lurched as if he were overcompensating. "Below the Oregon border on the coast. Laura's hometown. She started the trip there."

"So she did send it." So much for blaming a paralegal.

Juan hovered near the envelope, latex gloves poised to retrieve it. "Why does it have my address—*my* address with *his* name. How does she know my address?"

Arkelett said, "The firm has it on file."

"My address?" Juan blinked. "But how? Why?"

"You haven't been in contact with Laura lately?"

"No. As a discipline, I try not to think about it. About him. I would never call his lawyer. Never."

Juan was so shaken by the idea that he turned away, touching his hand to the snarling cheek of a candlelit gargoyle. Arkelett watched him.

When Juan turned back, Arkelett continued, "And except for the will, Laura hasn't been in touch with you?"

"Only through Castle. He's very much in touch with me. But not in the way you mean." Juan gestured toward the envelope. "This would be very crude for him. So blunt that at first I thought it was meant as an insult. But I begin to see the layers on top of layers."

"I expect I've stirred up a lot of worries, coming down here like this." Arkelett seemed to be memorizing every millimeter of the envelope. "But I'm just . . ." He glanced at me again. "Just trying to correct an office mistake, that's all. If I possibly can." He extracted the will.

Juan took a stumbling backward step, staring as if Arkelett had shaken out an appendage of Castle's. "I will go, go and . . . leave you for a moment."

He started pushing open the door to another room. Then he turned back to us, trotting to the whitewashed chair and scooting it behind Arkelett, virtually forcing him to sit. He left as if chased out.

Arkelett hunched over the will, giving it his full attention. I stood behind the chair, reading over his shoulder. Arkelett turned to me. "You don't know much about Castle's trial?"

"Only what Mr. Gomez told me."

He seemed on the verge of saying something difficult. Then, with a shake of the head, "I'm not clear enough on client confidentiality to know how much I can say now." As Di Palma's associate, he was obligated to keep her client matters confidential. "I don't know if Castle's acquittal changes anything. Especially these days, with civil suits getting filed after not-guilty criminal verdicts."

Was he about to admit Castle's guilt? I'd already gathered as much. But he was right, the double-jeopardy rule protected Castle only from criminal reprosecution. It offered no immunity from a civil suit. So it wouldn't do for Arkelett to confirm Castle's guilt. Nevertheless, I was silent, hoping he'd say more.

With a shrug, he continued, "You should read the court documents." A half smile. "And take a look at the arrest report and booking sheet."

Castle must have priors I should know about. Or maybe something in the records supported Juan's fears. Everyone was so damn odd about Castle. I was ready to invest in a few gargoyles myself.

Juan returned then. Arkelett slipped the will back into its envelope.

"Thanks for your time." Arkelett stood slowly. "And thank you, Ms. Jansson. I'm a hundred percent sure Laura's going to phone you first thing when she gets back."

"You'd better find your Ms. Di Palma soon," Juan advised.

Arkelett stopped moving.

"She never understood what Castle is," Juan continued. "She was like a woman with dust thrown in her eyes. When he can blind a woman, he can take her away from anyone. Like he took Becky away from me. He can make her do anything."

Arkelett's face drained of color. "Can you elaborate on that?"

Juan shrugged.

"Are you saying she's in some kind of physical danger?"

"Mental danger, spiritual danger." Juan's eyes glittered.

Arkelett watched him for a moment. "Laura knew what and who she was dealing with—it's not a matter of dust in her eyes. But a lawyer's got to do everything she can for her client. You understand that, don't you? That it was Laura's job to win an acquittal? That's not to say it's necessarily the best result, not even for Castle. Maybe sometimes it's better to put someone away where he can get treatment, even punishment. But from the point of view of the lawyer, she's obliged to go for the gold. That's her pact with the client. Whether it's right in the long run . . . that's for the client to decide, that's for God to know. Laura did her job, that's all. You do understand that?"

Juan stared at his gargoyles. "Yes." His voice was a whisper. "But maybe Becky doesn't understand."

Arkelett handed me the will and walked out.

Until Juan mentioned them, I don't suppose I'd ever thought about prophetic dreams. But that night, I believed I'd had one.

I dreamed I was sitting in Assistant District Attorney Patrick Toben's no-frills office. Toben was the only local ADA I knew. I'd recently tried a case against him.

In my dream, Toben, dapper and well-groomed as in life, wore a gargoyle print tie. "I called you," he said, "because your business card was found at the crime scene."

At that, I awakened suddenly and fully, convinced Juan Gomez was about to be killed by Sean Castle. My dark bedroom seemed thick with shapes, lurking like Castle's curse. *I'll kill you by inches, Juan. You'll see it coming for miles, so don't look back.*

I sat up, clicking on a lamp. My new place smelled of carpet shampoo and fresh paint. The walls were bare and the corners piled high with boxes. I could hear the clang of metal pulleys on masts at the nearby yacht harbor.

I crawled out of bed, clammy with fear. I pulled a jacket over the sweats I'd slept in, and I slipped into my moccasins. I started toward the door.

I stopped with my hand on the knob. I was still half-asleep, showing a dreamlike lack of impulse control. What excuse did I have for awakening Juan Gomez at this time of night? He was scared enough without having me appear on his doorstep to relate a nightmare.

I took a deep breath. I'd gotten sucked into Juan's world of dreams and curses, complete with medieval gargoyles to protect the sleeping. But I knew better than to elevate mere worries into voodoo, misgivings into prophecies. Sean Castle could manipulate Juan only because Juan had done the psychological and emotional spadework for him. Juan himself had created the pursued, cowering man Castle had vowed to make of him.

Juan said Castle would harm me, too, if he became aware of me. But I could see Juan had it backward. Castle could undermine me only if *I* became aware of *him,* only if I let myself dread what he might do to me. Only if I frightened myself enough to awaken a client in the middle of the night.

I returned to bed and huddled there, trying hard not to imagine gargoyles, claws outstretched, in the shadows beyond the lamplight.

I hugged myself against the seacoast chill, thinking about the tale Juan had told, replaying his words in my mind.

Having shared his horror, however briefly, I could move beyond smug pity. It scared me how much that seemed to change his story. Minutes before, I'd been proud of myself for breaking the chain of Juan's superstition. Now I feared the situation was much more complicated than that. How had Juan put it? *I want to wish it could be so simple.*

I considered Sandy Arkelett's reaction to Juan, his worries about revealing a client confidence, his advice that I read the court records and look at the booking sheet. I pondered the fact that Arkelett had recognized my name many years after my testimony, but hadn't recognized Juan's after only a year.

Once again, I jumped out of bed.

I cruised slowly past Juan's house, disquieted to see orbs of candlelight through his sagging curtains. It was nearly four in the morning. I'd hoped for the consolation of finding the place peaceful and dark.

I pulled up to the curb. I'd already promised myself: no debate. If Juan seemed to be stirring, I would knock no matter how foolish I felt. Maybe I had this figured wrong—unlike Di Palma, I made mistakes with disgusting frequency. Even if I was right, it was slim reason to bother Juan in the middle of the night.

But I just couldn't stop worrying about my dream. *Your card was found at the crime scene,* Assistant DA Toben had said.

Maybe it was a blessing not to be as perfect as Di Palma—I was used to apologizing. If I'd worried for nothing, fine, I would simply admit to being an idiot.

I looked over my shoulder as I approached the house. I'd feel like a flake persuading his neighbors I was no prowler.

When I knocked at the door, it opened slightly. Juan had left it unlocked, virtually ajar. Fear crawled up my spine. A man with gargoyles on every horizontal surface wouldn't leave his door open. Not unless he'd given up on protecting himself from Sean Castle. Not unless he'd tired of waiting in agonized dread.

I pushed my way in. "Juan?"

I almost stumbled over an object near the threshold. It was a gargoyle, shattered into lumps and shards of plaster as if dashed against the wall.

Only a few candles glowed, leaving most of the room in shadow. Whitewashed furniture picked up flickers of color from glass votives. There was barely enough light to make out the remains of other gargoyles, their pieces strewn as if in a berserk frenzy. Their cracked demon faces, portions of curling claws, and remnants of reptilian wings covered the floor like macabre carnage.

For a moment, I let myself believe that the large shadow in the corner was another gargoyle, still intact. But I approached it with a knot rising up my throat. I knew it was Juan Gomez, sprawled dead on the floor.

My business card, I noticed, was lying in a pool of blood beside his hand.

Sean Castle had smashed all the gargoyles. Then he'd slashed Juan's wrists with the jagged slivers of plaster. Or perhaps Juan, sure Castle was coming for him, had beaten him to the punch.

Exsanguination was listed as the cause of death. Suicide was presumed, despite the fact that Castle's fingerprints were all over the house.

I spent the rest of the night with the police. Then I went to the office of Assistant District Attorney Patrick Toben. Toben had prosecuted Sean Castle. Now he had the paperwork for this case.

It was only right that he should. My client, I had come to

realize, wasn't Juan Gomez, after all. He was Sean Castle.

"Yeah, Sean Castle killed Becky Walker, all right." Toben ran a hand over his neat ginger hair. "Walker was living with Castle in his cabin. We think she freaked out over something he did—probably showing multiple personalities. So he got self-protective and blew her head off. From what you just told me, I guess there was a Juan Gomez inside him watching the whole thing happen. Whatever. By the time we caught up to Castle, he'd ditched the clothes he'd been wearing, gotten rid of the weapon, everything. We just didn't have enough for a conviction. That's how Di Palma played it. You ever seen her in court? Well, then you know. She's good."

"The name Juan Gomez never even came up?"

"Di Palma never let a psychiatrist near Castle. She told us from day one she wasn't going to argue diminished capacity or insanity, nothing like that. She completely removed it as a trial issue, precluding us from examining him ourselves. And from what you tell me now, I can see why. If the psychiatrists labeled him a multiple, we'd have used it against him, we'd have looked for a violent personality or at least suggested the possibility. But our circumstantial case was weak enough that Di Palma stayed away from all of that. She was smart. She must have known, but she let it hang on whether we had enough proof."

I reached out a shaky hand for the coffee Toben had poured me. "When Sandy Arkelett saw Gomez—Castle—I could tell something wasn't right. But I assumed it had to do with Di Palma, with Arkelett trying to find her."

"It's a long drive to look at a postmark," Toben agreed.

"I suppose he just couldn't imagine Di Palma sending a will to a beneficiary by mistake. Sheesh, nobody would take time to check it out if I messed up. "He knew something was wrong."

"Looks like Di Palma didn't screw up, after all." Toben

didn't seem very pleased to say so. "I assume Castle had Di Palma write up his will, and that she mailed it to him while she was on the road."

I envisioned Castle receiving the will and writing "Juan Gomez c/o" above the address. He certainly knew how to scare his alter ego. By asking "Juan Gomez" to return to Walker's cabin, Castle was, in essence, making "Juan" assume responsibility, pointing out that he'd been present during the murder, too. Castle was reminding his better half, as it were, that the hand that killed Becky Walker belonged to both of them.

The real question was, had Castle killed "Juan?" Had he taken revenge on his cringing cohabitant? Or had "Juan" rid the world of Castle, killing Becky's murderer the only way he could?

"I should have known something was fishy as soon as I saw Arkelett's reaction to Castle," I fretted again. "He knew the score the minute the front door opened. He knew the problem wasn't with Di Palma, he knew she hadn't made a mistake with the address." I took a swallow of weak coffee. "I was so dense. Even when Arkelett told me to look up the arrest report."

"You'd have recognized Castle's booking photo." Toben tapped a pencil against a file folder.

"Arkelett could have just told me. The photo's a public record." But I knew Arkelett's reluctance involved not the photo but the conclusion to be drawn from it: that Sean Castle had multiple personalities, one of whom was willing to incriminate another. This wasn't an observation to be made by an associate of Castle's lawyer. Not in an era of civil trials following criminal acquittals.

I knew all that. But it didn't take the bitter taste out of my mouth. Maybe I could have done something if I'd figured this out sooner. I wished, not for the first time, that Di Palma and her PI weren't so damned competent.

"We talked to Di Palma this morning," Toben continued. "We tracked her down through an uncle—she's up north. She got real quiet when I told her what happened." His lips curled with disdain. "If she'd have let us do our jobs and put Castle away, he'd be a hell of a lot better off now."

And if Toben had presented a stronger case against Castle, Di Palma would have had to settle for an insanity or diminished capacity defense. But however she might feel about this result, Sandy Arkelett was right. She'd done everything she should for her client. She'd won him his freedom.

Then she'd left it to him to find real justice within himself and with his other selves.

I tried to remember what else "Juan" had told me about Castle. "Was he really a famous dream researcher?"

"Is that what he said?"

"Something about prophetic dreams. He had all those gargoyles to protect him while he slept."

"Sean Castle was the man you met in that little house. Did he look famous to you?"

"No. It's just that . . . I guess on some level, I figured this out while I was sleeping." I refused to attribute more than that to my dream. "I woke up in the middle of night worrying about it."

"That's why you went over there?"

I nodded. The police had obviously considered my nocturnal call bizarre. Toben probably agreed, but he didn't comment.

He said, "For a living, Castle did a bit of everything. Gardening, roto-rooting, worked at the canneries when they hired extras."

"Castle, gargoyles—I suppose it was just the association of ideas. Gargoyles protect Castles."

"I guess gargoyles aren't protection enough."

"Neither are lawyers, not even the best of them."